T0278519

An Old Carriage with Curtains

THE ARAB LIST

An Old Carriage with Curtains

GHASSAN ZAQTAN

TRANSLATED BY SAMUEL WILDER

LONDON NEW YORK CALCUTTA

The Arab List
SERIES EDITOR
Hosam Aboul-Ela

Seagull Books, 2023

© Ghassan Zaqtan, 2011
English translation © Samuel Wilder, 2023

ISBN   978 1 8030 9 234 8

British Library Cataloguing-in-Publication Data
A catalogue record for this book is available from
the British Library.

Typeset by Seagull Books, Calcutta, India
Printed and bound in the USA by Integrated Books International

An Old Carriage with Curtains

He turned right into the narrow pass, Khal al-Ahmar was behind him now. Having veered off the fast road, he found himself facing the wadi. He was wrapped in the strange energy of the place, lost in dark over-laps of severity and astonishment, overtaken by something like a deep mercy under everything that folded with assurance over the broken rocks and downslopes marking the dark course of the river.

A narrow road stretched through the wadi, twisting in elevation above the river and the stone walls that follow its edges. Green merged thickly out of the darkness. Bushes, silhouettes of trees and small thorny brush rose out of the chasm, branches hung confidently in the hollow space filled by the sound of water dropping in darkness, the only sound that marked the scene. A terror quickly gripped him as he sighted the stone lines that enclosed the monastery of Saint George, built on top of a way-station for the travellers who passed on this rugged, dangerous, ancient road five centuries before the life of the monk George Huseini. The monastery came into view, its dome suspended in the mountain like a strung orthodox icon.

Why might you stand here, listening to the call of minor miracles huddling in the strange powers of the wadi?—the angel Bashir Joachim wandering in the wilderness with Mary, giving the monastery its miraculous power to bestow blessings and the gift of pregnancy; Ilya's flight from the oppression of King Ahab, the crows that brought him his bread and meat every morning; Christ drinking from the spring next to where the monastery was built, passing the wadi on his way to Jericho; the stories that turn all that exists here in this web of small miracles, each like a miniscule jinni set to the lure the passers-by.

The road where he stood was the ancient path between Jericho and Jerusalem. In the darkness of the rock formations and downslopes of hills, he could make out the voids of caves. These, he thought, were the same caves where monks had found refuge in the early years of Christianity's persecution. He was enveloped now by the wadi, its caves and rock formations, its strange intractable places, sweet springs and the dark power that had protected the monks and isolated their worship. The low, slowed sound of falling water, the strange plants and birds, the fish flying over fault lines in the earth so close to the desert, it all seemed like a momentary, divine gift.

He shuddered to think that he walked now in the 'valley of the shadow of death'. The fear that gripped him was undiminished by the miracles of the monastery, the wadi's power to yield protection and isolation, and the herds of travellers that arrived in blue buses; by the children of the bedu who shouted cheerfully and climbed the stone walls by fixing ropes on the edges of the stones; and even by the two women travellers, most likely Germans, who stood now in front of the doorway snapping pictures of the bodies of the playing boys.

The story said that when the Persians despoiled the wadi on their way to Jerusalem, they slaughtered the ascetics in the caves, five thousand of them, including fourteen monks inside the halls, whose skulls were now kept in the monastery.

He tried to place it all in front of him now. An invading army that climbed the white hills and green fields into the mountains, following the course of the agitated water, pushing the birds and mountain foxes in front of them, soldiers panting and yelling at the openings of caves, and on the thresholds and steps of the monastery. Amid the exaggerations of this missionary narrative, there was still a silent element, the monks, to whom he could give no voice or cry to mark their fates.

This all came to completion as he arrived at the first steps rising to the monastery of Saint George.

More than thirty years ago, in Jabal al-Taj, the neighbourhood east of Amman, he had stopped in front of a poster on the door of a carpenter's workshop, cheap and hastily printed in black and white. It showed the pictures of sixteen young men, the youngest, he thought, around fourteen years old. At the top of the poster, above the pictures, was a broad printed title, 'Martyrs of the Battle of Wadi al-Qalat'. In smaller print were details about the battle, a long-winded explanation lionizing the dead young men, removing none of obscurity of this battle.

Since then, Wadi Qelt had signified a dark passage through low thorn bushes and wounding stones, filled by a monotonous sound of water falling in darkness.

Since that morning, he had found himself running behind the wadi with no end to his questions. He asked his geography teacher, his older sister and his father if he returned home early in a good mood. He asked Ahmad, the boastful boy in his class whose father had emigrated from the camp to Germany, seeking work. He gathered pictures, maps and tourist prints left behind by pilgrims passing through the camp on their way to celebrate Epiphany at the Jordan River. All of this material he collected in a small tin sweets box, into which he also put the travellers' descriptions that he found in the books of his often-absent father, along with newspaper clippings where the wadi was mentioned. It was in a story in one of the missionary books that he came across the massacre of the monks. The killing of the sixteen youths later melded into this. These stories overflowed in this place darkly, mixing into the narrative of the isolation and death of the monks.

The wadi was outside the box now, outside the scraps and pictures, fissuring open, breathing and panting in a painful, constant fall towards the lowland. It looked more impassable, cruel, anxious than anything he had imagined that morning in Amman, sweeping beyond what he had sketched from the piles in the box. None of the wadi's impassibility was tempered by his passage to this point on foot. Its confusion and darkness remained, yielding only some confused glimmers of expectation between rock faces, hopes that some secrets might still come to light—some light on the dead youths, their lithe bodies and neutral black-and-white faces, or some light on the monks' frocks that disappeared in the dark cavities of the watercourse.

The wadi started next to Jerusalem, in the village of Anata, which bore the name of the Canaanites' Goddess Anatut, their goddess of war, love and the hunt. The narrative in the Torah gave a brief indication that King Solomon used to hunt and walk in these hills. But what did Solomon hunt in these hills, the king gifted to speak to the birds and animals?

In their time, the Byzantines had called it Anato. The Syriac-Arameans called it Anatiya.

He loved to trace the names of the villages and wadis, to revolve and etch their names through the ages that had passed over this land. It was a passion that started in his search for the name of their village. Zakariyya. It began up on the hill, four thousand years ago, when it was called Azkaah or Aziika, a name that came from the planting and tilling of the earth. It then moved, he thought, from the peak of the great hill bearing its name, down into the plain and the wadis around it, which were all named after trees. Wadi al-Sant, Wadi Butm where David took on Goliath, Dahr al-Kandul, and Wadi Bulis with its small shrine of the prophet who had that name. The wadis with their names and alterations were like living, speaking beings, he thought, as he continued to descend in Wadi Qelt down to its vanishing point in the plain of Jericho, where the ruins of Herod's castle spread like wings on the wadi's flanks, just south of the faded remnants of the royal garden.

Water cascaded from the stones to form a strange brook running into the Dead Sea, transforming, he thought, as if coloured by the cries of the Persian troops, inmixed with blood dripping from the sixteen boys more than thirty years ago.

As he continued the journey towards west of Jericho, he passed beyond the wadi and the monastery of Saint George, leaving the bodies of the young men stretching in the bends of the wadi. The massacre of the monks, the strange birds, wonders and plants of the afterlife, all continued their life behind him, as the air became heavy, pressing his chest, shoulders and eyes as he descended the river course below the sea level. He felt as if he joined some eternal waterfall, a companion that had waited for him for ever, encircling him now—armies, monks, raiders, plants, birds, water, scents, voices cherished like amulets, invocations, instincts; sixteen youths, women, horses, horses, foxes, hyenas, prophets holding miracles, miracles in search of prophets who had not yet found guidance; believers, the lost, the poets, philosophers, the sculptors and weavers, the mills and cane presses and fishermen; stags and tax collectors, priestesses, temples, a pale moon; the fences and prayers, betrayal and trumpets; and a lone adulteress left in the story like a puzzle.

This was his company as the water poured, vaunting its grandeur, constantly renewing itself, like some tremendous line of darkness and light, as he dropped below the sea level in his passage towards Jericho.

He felt something like the fulfilment of a promise deferred so long it was forgotten. His stubbornness and his submission drove him on. He knew he had to climb Mount Qarantal, whose southern face was marked by caves and caverns, as if the massacre itself had somehow slipped and fallen from the story and set out in pursuit of the mountain itself.

If he turned his eyes upward and blocked the glare of the sun, he could make out the monastery's chambers suspended in the stone walls above him, just as they had been more than thirty years before, as if drawn on the mountain by a child's hand.

He climbed, following the temple path, towards a narrow entrance that led onto a trodden dirt pass climbing the cliff-face towards the monastery near the summit. While the sun climbed in the east, another burning day rose to meet first the naked white hills and salt surface of the lake, then the knoll of palms and the banana fields at its base, the earthen houses and the trench stretching between the two mountain chains. Thick blue mist above obscured the distant scene of Jerusalem.

Jericho, like an explosion of sudden green, gathered in sight of the monastery. He thought of its ancient fears, this first city to fortify itself.

When he knocked on the monastery door, a small aperture opened. Behind it appeared the pale face of a nun, perhaps Greek, who spoke in starkly brief Arabic: 'No visitors today.'

All he wanted to see was the tomb, the monastery's tomb where they had buried the monks who had ascended in order to sever their worldly ties, whose sole concern on this earth was to behold the messiah in those dark halls penetrating the heart of the mountain.

They came to the mountain one by one, leaning into their prayers and their absolute benevolence, a benevolence that took them with outstretched hands to the most extreme realm of life, where they could look out over death and coexist, or at least to glimpse it in the narrow passages and barren rooms where they moved with light steps and hushed voices.

He wanted to know for sure that the tomb existed, and perhaps to complete the school trip he had begun decades earlier when he had gone, along with four other boys, all the way up to the monastery gate. They had walked the narrow pass up to the highest point in the wadi. He had not forgotten their tiny faces and their shaved heads that bowed to the strictures of the UN agency school they attended, which was set up to care for the refugees until they could return to the homes, fields and jobs they had left in the 'war'.

He still had their picture preserved in the case. Taken by their teacher, Ismail, it showed the students in the fifth grade of primary school. Ismail had gathered all the participants of the monastery trip under a great poinciana tree on the streets of Jericho and taken the photograph himself, then sent a copy to each of them at the end of the year.

He remembered the boys now, squatting in the front row of the picture, stuck together in a single clump, displaying their shaven heads and flashing eyes. They overlapped now in his memory with the faces of the sixteen youths on the poster. He thought of each of their fates, and tried to recall their names. He had a lingering fear that he might be the only one left now, still trying to bring that journey to an end.

The door did not open to their knocks at first, but they kept standing in front of the monastery, boyish and obstinate, as the scorching sun wasted their bodies until even the desire to enter for a small drink of water was exhausted, ravaging them with thirst in front of the locked door on the exposed landing of the mountainside.

The strong noon sun spread over where they stood. The Dead Sea shone like an enormous old brass mirror. Then the door opened, and a young monk appeared. He took them into shade within the entrance. A nun came out of the darkness to offer glasses of water, as the kind monk spoke in laboured Arabic, placing his hands on the boy's sun-warmed, bare heads. The monk was so kind that they could not question him, especially about the tomb.

The nun peering from the aperture thirty years later—whom he thought, for some reason, seemed Greek—did not wait for him to put a question or explain what he wanted. She closed the aperture once her decisive sentence was completed: 'No visitors today.'

In the vast silence, he heard steps becoming distant on a path inside the mountain.

The lake on the plain, its dry banks and the flashing salt islets that pierced its heavy water, presented some absurd polar scene. To the east, a line of dark greenery obscured the glimmering river, whose sharp turns he could guess at only by following the line of dark green, behind which he imagined the worried course and turbid waters of the river. Behind him, the trench fanned out along the sides of the mountain. The scene appeared to him now like a lesson in history or geography that had leapt out of a book, and was breathing in front of him. Now he could rearrange the narrative. He could see the paths and movements of his heroes, on the shores of the lake, in the passes in the Balqa mountains, and in the wadis that shed their winter waters into the river. His eyes could trace the white hills that fall away in the ascent west of Jerusalem.

He stood in front of the closed aperture, alone in the burning heat of the noon sun, remembering the monk's hand on his warm, bald head more than thirty years earlier. He had never told the monk his unslaked desire, to see the tomb of the monks. The desire remained with him today.

It is the first time he had returned to the monastery door, he thought, since he had come back *here*. Although the idea of climbing to the monastery had never left him, he had found excuses always, to put it off. He had overwhelmed by the idea of making all the arrangements required, to finally come back *here*. As he walked, his memories piled beside him, amassing as if threshed by some churning mower. The dead and the living all walked beside him, a caravan in which no one dies and no one arrives. The mower pushed it all into the pile beside him, all of them, places and fates, their dreams and mistakes. The lives they lost. It seemed that it could all be some enormous, meaningless exaggeration.

As he descended towards Jericho in Wadi Qelt, the ineluctable course of the river made sharp turns through water-carved stone. A feeling came back that had long disappeared. He felt again he was journeying in his own memories. He felt he had to return to these memories, to give them some arrangement. The beings the journey gave him, he could bring them back.

Intensely and slowly, he brought back his old, overlapping belongings, the things whose absence had discomposed his memory and pulled it apart like a straw mat.

It was after he came back *here* that he began to place his belongings, his memories, into a new box. He put them all in: the wadi and its dead, the monasteries and crows; Hind, with her stories and the laugh that he found obscene; the Israeli woman soldier, who seemed Russian, and all her silent gestures; the dialects, the roads and the Moroccan Jewish woman who owned the cafe—all the things that will be mentioned now. *Here* had grown heavy, necessary, strong. The place came to powers nourished in its shadows.

He had to begin at some event, some event that he might enter, to describe and change it, something he could tell as a story with an ending. They are not prophecies, but events, that seem to happen *here*, even as prophecies flood in from the mist in their complete forms, firm and eternal. He started with the fates of persons, and their intentions. He followed them as they laboured through the trivial facts of their lives. He prodded them into appearance on the roads and in the houses, or scattered through the humble fields.

He did not know where to start, or if the strands would yield to be woven together, but he knew, painfully, that *here* everything leads to everything. They all passed through the 'valley of the shadow of death' without protection.

The Bridge and the Fat Man Who Cut in Line

From his place in line, he could see the woman soldier seated behind the checkpoint glass, totally busy,
shuffling the papers and permits of a family—a
father, mother and five children. The father, mechan-
ically following her requests, picked up one of the
boys and lifted him to the checkpoint so that she
could juxtapose him with the papers between her
hands. At the same time, the mother tried to keep
the movements of the other children under control,
preparing them to take the hands of their father. She
looked like a girl impatiently wrapping a coloured
veil.

He started to count again. There were still nine
people in front of him. She was slow, he thought, and
deliberately so, and she would certainly take even
more time with the two young men in line behind
the family. They always take more time with young
men.

The father then lifted the smallest boy. He heard her pose a question in broken Arabic, which he could only make out in the pronunciation of the child's name.

Yusuf, the father said. Yusuf was swung by his arms to the checkpoint, his face submissive and astonished, looking at the woman soldier behind glass.

He noticed the constant drone of the electronic gate in the hall's entryway, where another line formed, headed by an old man. The old man, with intense caution, was trying to walk through the electronic gate, encircled by signage, beside the cart given to him by the Arab worker at entry. The woman soldier behind glass raised her voice impatiently as voices from the line encouraged him. The armed intelligence officer to the left of the gate watched the man labour to lay down his silver-gilded walking stick, which he set into the cart as if giving it final burial.

Focussed intently on how to enter this machine gate, the man looked back and forth at the line behind him, where expressions of encouragement were rising. The woman soldier kept shouting and gestured with her hands behind the glass. He glanced also at the silver-gilded walking stick as it vanished into the machine next to him.

He watched the old man's awkward hand movements and the confusion that washed across his face, devoid now of the confidence that had brought him from the door of his home to the machine gate. Standing here, he forgot his hands, which fled somewhere else, painfully emptied.

As he expected, the short young man was sent back to the seat to await security inspection. He went to the seat promptly, as if he had crossed the hall a thousand times, to sit quietly opposite one of the locked gates. It was clear the young man had been here before, that he knew this seat, hallway, and door. The command he had been given was a fragment, a mere hand signal, but the youth had magically unwrapped it, had furnished the seemingly innocent spontaneous sign with its details. As if by some trick, the gesture sent him on a passage to the seat next to the walls and door. The second young man, the taller one, stood behind the checkpoint now. He looked confused and lost.

The family was now in line at the doorway leading to the bus, like a line of explorers in single file. The father was at the head, then the five children according to their heights, then the mother at the end of the line to keep the children from straying off. The father called to the children and brought each of them in turn to face a second female soldier, who revolved their papers and checked for stamps. Yusuf pulled at his mother's dress.

He made sure to wait behind the yellow line as they processed the fat man in front, who had snuck up to cut the line, pretending to greet a friend. He had no desire to argue with him, unlike the younger woman at the back of the line. Instead, he chose to spend his time looking at the woman soldier. The fat man's petty manoeuvre only granted him more time to do that. As he took all of this in, the young woman in jeans at the back of the line went on complaining about the fat man. But the fat man just stood there unfazed, ignoring her protests.

The young complaining woman reminded him of Hind. Or, more precisely, the performance and dialect of the complaining, and all the ambiguous laughter that followed, hurdled her into his mind. Hind. He had never figured out what she desired from him.

Perhaps that was why he kept to his role as a silent, curious listener in their strange relationship.

He sat before her wide-eyed, looking on dispassionately, between them were two small glasses of coffee, a brass coffee pot, an ashtray full of cigarette butts, some of which were streaked with red lipstick. She spoke with her hands, eyes, chest and body, as he fought to keep his imagination away from finding an entirely different scene. In her effusions he could deduce almost nothing. It all felt rushed and spontaneous. There was a strain of violence in how she moved. Only the perpetual exhaustion beneath her eyelids revealed that she was not ten years younger. There was madness in her laugh. Her speech was direct. She brought out images and similes that were shockingly common, she let curses walk through the folds of her talk like a row of departing camels.

He tried to take it all in, but strained to close the windows in his imagination that she ceaselessly opened. She surged through her shirt in outrageous laughter, her chest uncovered, telling never-ending stories, moving off in all directions with no pauses, dropping signs that he would find wherever he went. At every turn, every road sign, stories and similes waited for him. In this net of signs, he found the stories that would follow him, up the mountain as he walked to the monastery, or down as he dropped in the wadi below the sea level; the stories that met him as he re-arranged his library to clear space for the studio portrait of his mother taken in Bethlehem, or the old, faded black-and-white picture of his village, Zakariyya, which had been carefully hidden on the second shelf of his mother's closet. The picture had become a family icon, treasured to the point that relatives even crossed long stretches between refugee camps to look at it. It had been taken, he thought, sometime after their displacement, but before the village was destroyed and the remaining members of her family fled to Ramla. In line now among the others, he seemed to hear Hind's voice as he held up his travel papers to the irritated Israeli soldier with her Slavic features.

When I crossed the Allenby Bridge for the first time, I was thirty-five. I had a small rucksack. I had taken the wrong passage, went down the wrong hallway, I think. You know I can't keep track in those mazes. The Israeli soldier called out to me, trying to be polite, you know how they always seem to be trying to be polite. I looked at his face and his weapon, his uniform and obvious irritation. He just repeated his one Arabic sentence that started with 'Madame'. He really leant into 'Madame,' then he finished it with: 'Right this way, if you please.'

Did you notice 'madame' and 'if you please'?! A person in full military fatigue and helmet, holding and an American M16 rifle, with its butt at your eyes, addressing you.

'Madame, right this way, if you please!'

The effort he had put into memorizing this sentence multiplied as he repeated it. He clung to it as if it gave him the right to send me back to my place.

His Arabic was butchery, the pronunciation of the consonants was terrible, yet the sentence somehow freed him from having to speak to me. It consummated any relationship he might have had with the white salt hills around us, the short dusty palms dotting the space around him or even with ancient Jericho.

He caressed his gun involuntarily, and after uttering the massacred sentence, he looked lost. Then he repeated it, sustaining its syllables as if to beg for some connection to the language.

Then, concluding, she turned to him directly: 'Believe me, we deserve better enemies than these ...'

When she raised from the fat man's papers to look him over, her eyes narrowed. It seemed for a moment that she was trying to remember him. The fat man kept on thanking her, needlessly, maybe trying to ingratiate her with his weak Hebrew, as she looked at him. Once the fat man moved on, he found himself faced with her eyes.

The Way to Zakariyya

He arrived late to Zakariyya, his village, occupied since 1948, where his father and mother were born. Somewhere in a drawer inside the house there was a faded, tormented picture that redeemed nothing, but which kept in place the stories that amassed in the family home. The picture showed a distant spectre of forest trees, and the ghosts of houses at the far-right edge of the frame. This was all it contained. It looked tired, faded, closed; nonetheless, it asserted some incredible forbearance. Under the pressure of the cruel importance placed on it, it could hardly go on existing, pressed down by the dependence of all those contradictory memories, all the longing that pervaded their stories.

Zakariyya was more than any one scene. The father built his narrative on the road, the woods, the sea's edge guarded by the hill. The uncle's narrative existed inside the tomb of the prophet Zakariyya, in a recurring dream, between sleep and waking, about the gathering of the jinn under it's the tomb's arches. Both were dead now, no one was left to remember all these things, the present consciousness of a speaker for those narratives was gone. No more marriages of the jinn or precise descriptions of celebrating spirits, no more narrow, thorny forest roads skipped across like fault lines, no boys to climb the hill and see the faint edge of the sea. They were children once, but they had died.

The narration of his mother was built on descriptions not narrative, so it seemed more precise. It lacked any boasting its text was mostly silence and absence, short sections of improvised songs, small asides between images consumed with courtyard details, upper rooms, low thresholds, or the captivated story of the man who always chased his lover's trail through the narrow trails, dousing her steps with vials of perfume that he had acquired in Jaffa.

The stories in the books go far beyond. The village first grew between the hill, the tomb and the ruins at the edges of the plain. There had been so many people and creatures. One could barely imagine how the ground could contain all these gods and armies. The Canaanites chose the hill overlooking the coastal plain for their called Azkaah, and they built something like a fort to shield the depths of the land from the exhausted armies of the Pharaohs that rose from the south through Gaza. It had been the last site to fall in the conquest of Sennacherib the Assyrian. Joshua arrived to this hill, from which one could see Goliath and the army of the Philistines gather in the valley, and the sieging armies of Nebuchadnezzar the Babylonian. After the Babylonian captivity, the village continued its life, lingering on the hillside up closer to the summit, then it descended a bit when the Roman army arrived. Its name then became Kaffar Zakariyya. It watched the Muslim armies arrive to the plain, burying their dead, then fanning across rivers and cities to the north. This humble place of burial later became the Salihi Tomb. The crusaders entered Palestine much later, then the village became a Syrian Orthodox possession, and a church for Mary Magdalene was built on the plain, before the armies of Saladin returned, taking the village down to its current point of settlement. When the Mamluk sultans of Egypt arrived, they apportioned it among the properties belonging to the Tomb of Ibrahim

Khalil in Jericho, once Hulagu Khan's armies were defeated.

Within this history a text that always held his fascination was the Testament of Abu Bakr, the declaration proclaimed by the army of Amr Ibn al-Aas when it first entered Palestine:

> *Do no treachery, inflict no extremes, no delusion, do not deceive; do not slay small children or elderly sheikhs, or women; do not hamstring or burn the date palms, do not fell the fruit trees . . . you will come across peoples who have gone off to hermitages, summon them and the objects of their devotion.*

He loved this admonishing declaration. He had memorized it out of a book that he read in the sixth grade. He loved how it brought together the trees and animals, delineating them as it walks above the army like a cloud. He cherished the strange ambiguity of the date palms, where the date palms are mentioned not like trees, but like something that can be 'hamstrung', in some confusion between tree and camel. The trees were carried out of their species, and given breath, a heart and legs. He recalled this speech when he learnt of massacre of the monks in

Wadi Qelt in the missionary book that he kept in his case. But he loved, still, the phrase that ended the declaration: *So we did not do that.*

Once he had asked an old Jewish man in the village, an occupier whom he guessed was Iraqi or Moroccan, who was sitting on a bench among ancient trees near the Salihi Tomb, where the Muslims had buried their dead in the Battle of Ajnadayn. Baffled, the old man shook his shoulders, then answered, 'I don't know. Did you say the Salihi Tomb? All of them left, there are none here. The ones who stayed were displaced to Ramla. Some of them do come to visit. We don't know their names. They wander through the streets, they sit on benches, they go to the mosque to pray, until the police come to send them away. Did you say the Salihi Tomb?'

On the main, fast road, there was a squirrel crushed by a speeding vehicle. A strange sight, since there were no squirrels in the stories that he knew. He did not think there were squirrels around here, but he'd heard them described adoringly in other, faraway places. This dead creature on the fast road near Zakariyya, it was certainly a squirrel.

For some reason, maybe to preserve his grasp on the story, he imagined the squirrel to have crept out of some neighbouring story, not the woods next to the road.

The village had not been destroyed as much as the surrounding towns. But the family houses from the fading family picture were completely obliterated. Only the abandoned tomb of the prophet Zakariyya, which gave the village its name, and the house of one of his uncles were still standing. On the slopes of the hills, one could see the remnants of lines of stones. These were the remains of walls of great unpolished stone, old, muttering signs that told secrets.

This is basically all there was.

During his return, he thought about whether any of this was necessary. The exhausted picture, corresponding to his memory of the village, seemed stronger and more durable than the village itself. It all seemed strange, cruel, full of prejudice.

Even colour photographs, taken with such professional skill, were powerless: the picture of his uncle's house, or the one taken within the tomb's hall that showed the crook and edge of the window, the shadow of an unknown tree; the picture of the school, which had become a workshop for repairing farm equipment. None of these other pictures held a descriptive power worth desiring, none sustained the degree of longing that he felt was captured in the faded image on the second shelf of his mother's closet. This is why he never sent them to her, as he had promised to do in his last visit to Amman, where she lived.

His third attempt to obtain a Visitation Permit, so that he could go see her, was proceeding well.

It would be issued soon, the Office of Connections said.

'There is no reason for them to refuse your request, but also they very rarely grant them,' said the Arab office worker, in his state of multiplying boredom behind the inquiries window, where he took up the requests to be conveyed to the occupation officers in the inner rooms.

As long as they have not refused it yet, then the matter is proceeding well, he had been told by someone reviewing the application, with a cold confidence that surprised him.

He supposed that this episode started long ago, more precisely in the fall of 1994. That was when he crossed from Gaza to Ramallah, carrying a Permission of Passage to enter Israel, a document that allowed him to cross between the two cities. He was permitted a duration of six hours, with the allowed course of passage specified in the margin. The driver of the car that he hired at Erez Checkpoint was a Palestinian living in Ramla. The regulations at the checkpoint and the delays initiated by the soldiers had already eaten up two of his hours; still, his exasperation was eased when the driver, standing on the other side of the checkpoint, agreed to drive him to Ramallah. It took him more than twenty minutes to select his driver, as he wanted an Arab driver, and it was not easy to make this distinction among the drivers who were all grouped around the makeshift table erected in the cafeteria. He heard the man say something into his mobile phone in Arabic, seemingly to his wife, about making it home late that night, and whether she should take the children for a visit. He approached and asked if he would take him to Ramallah.

On the road, stories began to appear surreptitiously, things he imagined were long forgotten appeared in reborn voices, gestures and sounds. He asked the man about their town, whether it was within the allowed boundaries of his passage. The driver took his permit to read over its details, then looked at his watch. Without comment, he turned into a narrow side road. After half an hour among wooded fields, on a road bordered by dark-green cypresses, the driver pointed to a road sign that showed the new Hebrew name of the village, Kaffar Zakariyya, spelt out in both Arabic and Hebrew. He looked at the sign. The name has remained, he thought. But in Hebrew, the name seemed muted, dulled and deliberate, devoid of the powers of spontaneous suggestion he saw in the curving Arabic letters.

The driver asked if this was the first time that he came this way. 'Yes,' he replied.

He never saw the village during that passage. The driver slowed down as much as he could, but couldn't find the street that branched off from the fast road and led towards the plaster-roofed houses. He could not spot the tomb's minaret beside the

35

square, which was in front of the hill that bore the remains of the school, now a workshop for repairing farm equipment, as the river told him.

Then Zakariyya was gone, as suddenly as it had appeared, once they turned into the dense thicket that rose on the sharp hillside. The road came back rushing, wide and straight.

At a paved clearing next to the road, the driver stopped the car. A coffee shop suddenly appeared, a small rest station with a name displayed in Hebrew on a wooden sign constructed from a country fence. The sign pointed to a narrow, wooden step bridge leading to the entrance.

'You can smoke and get good coffee here,' the driver said, pointing to the coffee shop at the entrance to the woods. 'The owner is Moroccan and she speaks Arabic,' as he stepped out of the car.

The two of them sat on the side facing the road, as the woman, in her forties, brought them coffee. She seemed to be friends with the driver. She joined them. Gesturing to him, she said, 'Your friend looks Moroccan.'

'He did live there for a while,' the driver said smiling.

The woman looked at him, then turned to speak directly into his eyes.

'Did you stay in Marrakech?'

'No, but I visited more than once.'

She turned to talk again to the driver.

'You must go there one day, Hasan, you will see a place that looks like nothing else. Marrakech is Marrakech! Then come back here so we can talk about Marrakech,' she said as she was rising.

'Just give me the key to your house there, and you'll find it all arranged when you decide to come back.'

The driver, whose name was Hasan, said this dispassionately.

She put her hand on his shoulder, her bracelets falling against his shirt. Her slowness now crept into his body, there was a confusion of scents as the perfume. The jasmine and incense in her hair passed over his hand and chest, and over the table.

'Is he your relative?'

'No, we're not related. I am taking him to Ramallah,' Hasan answered, staring into the grove propped on the mountain side. 'But we are from the same village.'

First Appearance of the 'Railway Station'
in Mother's Story

Sometime later, he described the journey to his mother. As if in the act of tearing through colourful gift wrapping, he lost himself in the description of the road and the woods, the great hill and the bend that led to the coffee shop and its Moroccan owner, the driver Hasan, and his surprise when he learnt he was from their village. Then she cut him off.

'Did you see the railway station?'

There were no trains, railway tracks or stations in his description. His story seemed to vaporize at this sudden interjection.

'The rail in Artouf,' she went on. 'They used to get down from the train, then make the rest of the way on horseback or foot. Only the hill separated us from the railway tracks, which ran down from the woods to the platform. We could hear the whistle from the house. The horse always jumped and reared when it heard the whistle.' This was the first time the train station entered her stories, of which it became like a secret key. From this point on, everything that he witnessed and sought to describe and remember for her, it all felt like only empty carriages with old, dusty curtains. It was not convincingly alive, because the railway station was gone. Its absence diffused through life, evaporating everything.

A Simple Need to Speak

Three weeks earlier, the woman soldier had asked if he liked to travel. The question was inappropriate and completely unexpected. He had replied, 'Yes.'

She flipped though his many stamps, then, handing back the papers, she muttered, 'Enjoy.'

For him it was a harsh departure from the agreement with *them* that had been in place now for decades. For a moment, he could not shake the deep bitterness that now joined him on the journey.

She had had transgressed her limits, he thought, confronting him with such neutrality. She should not be offering wishes on his behalf. She had crossed a sacred threshold.

It was the first time that one of the workers on the Bridge, one of *them*, had confronted him with as neutral expression such as 'Do you like to travel?' or 'Enjoy.'

Things were kept clear and appropriate, a clean, total distance was maintained. The endless complications and infuriating procedures were included in this agreement, and the only thing that allowed for anything close to relaxation was the fact that they did all of these things in order to become and remain *them*—that was their role, just as our role was to accommodate, to continue to stare over their shoulders towards wherever we need to go.

He liked to think about *them* on the Bridge just as *they* were, cocky adolescent boys and sullen, impatient young women, enacting a petulant, imperial occupation. This all rested on the fact that they would one day leave, that one would no longer see them hopping like grasshoppers through the hallways and rooms of this passage. It was for that reason alone, because he could think in this way, that he could bear them.

The idea that they were temporary put them at a distance and removed their particularities. They all looked alike to him, even the young Ethiopian Falash woman, even the soldier who seemed to be from an Arab background, who stood next to the Ethiopian woman as she looked on with seeming admiration, making all efforts to copy them, to become one of them, redoubling her efforts to make up for her skin, which was as dark as that of the Ghawarina Palestinian workers who also worked on the Bridge. Absorbed in her desire to resemble them, she worked with pitiable determination, striving not to be linked to the Palestinian construction and sanitation workers. Stirred with melancholic pity, he watched her, as he always did when he crossed the Bridge. He felt more for her than he did for the Palestinian workers who worked so hard to please the cocky and sullen soldiers, but who never dared attempt the further step towards resemblance.

His role in the agreement was also clear to him—to pass curtly, intensely silent, not to grumble, to let all matters proceed in a way that one can get accustomed to, to hold to his silent and calm aversions, to look at *them* as temporary strangers, affirm everything and uphold a complete pretension of ignorance.

That is why it shocked him when she crossed the threshold with her severe aberration, a meaningless contextless expression, free of all that had been constructed and accumulated.

Maybe she had absently noted that he had shown her his papers numerous times in quick succession, without the security apparatus rejecting them. Maybe she wanted to tell him, *We* are following your travels.

This possibility might have seemed best suited to explain the context, except for the way she looked at him, which revealed some painful other thing, as if she were saying, Oh, me too.

It seemed to come from a basic desire to speak.

You Don't Look Like Your Mother and
You Don't Seem Angry Enough

'Did I tell you where my aunt Zakiyya died?' Hind asked suddenly, without lifting her eyes from the framed picture of his mother that hung on the opposite wall.

'It doesn't matter how, but where she died.'

'In Wavell.'

'Do you know what Wavell is?' '

It is the name of the place where Zakiyya died. It is named after a French soldier who arrived in Lebanon and encamped in a fortress near Baalbek. It is a true fortress, surrounded by high walls and a fortified gate, with towers and turrets. Inside, the structure is divided into quarters of officers' housing, sleeping barracks for the troops, stables for the horses and storehouses for weapons, rations and supplies. The lower floors contain long rows of narrow prison cells, into which the resisting Arabs of Syria and Lebanon were driven. Executions took place in the main hall, which overlooks the Beqaa Valley. You could see the foothills at the base of the mountain chain, and the road to Damascus stretching past Zahleh and Chtoura. That is where Zakiyya went, among the exhausted people of the villages of the north, after she had wandered on the road and joined one of the caravans moving north, while her family went east towards Jordan. That is where they put them. The fortress was named al-Jaleel, but no one took this name seriously, it kept its name as Camp Wavell.

Zakiyya—I prefer to call her by her name—lived in one of the cells until she died, alone, more than forty years later. On the night of her death, I went down the dark hallway on lower level. There were damp, decomposing smells and the breath of people sleeping. The smell led me towards the cell where she lived. The cell was hers alone, but she had invited three little girls to sleep there when their families' cells became too cramped.

I sat on the ground at the threshold, across from the cell window, which made a small spot of darkness on the wall. I did not cry with the other women.

Her death was deep and violent. Shrouded under the window, she was a pale, slender old woman surrounded by the sobbing and laments of women she did not know. In the middle of this, there was some controversy over possession of the now-vacant cell, even as the three small girls stared at the dead body with staggered sadness.

Desolation, as it enveloped her, overcame me too. It was not her death, but her isolation, the seclusion of her terrifyingly gaunt body. I do not know if you will believe me when I tell you, but I heard her voice say, 'Do not die alone.'

The shrouded body said this to me under the window. Something like this. Maybe that was why I did not cry, because we were speaking behind their backs. Somehow it seemed she said, 'Do you see, there is no good in waiting and remembering. Waiting moves no air. Children's clothes do not grow in boxes. The things we love do not happen here. Try to be *there* instead. Do not die in the darkness.'

On that night I decided to come back here. Somewhere in the darkness of the place others negotiated around us, they reckoned lists and names. My name spun like a roulette wheel with four quadrants.

It was raining when an exhausted guard locked the fortress gate behind me. I started to breathe, feeling them all behind me now, behind the wall, the towers and the iron gateway, beyond the cells' windows, arranging their lives and distributing plots for the dead. They split into a doubled image: prison and exile, with a window in between. Prison is also exile, exile also prison—in Wavell, the window is gone. It's one.

She seemed to reach the end of her speech. She is loving this, he thought. All she needed was a pulpit and an audience—and he could give her the latter. She rose from her seat to face the pictures hung on the wall. She looked at the picture of his mother taken in the studio in Bethlehem, her posture and the careful decorations of the photographer. His mother looked confidently into the camera; a minimal smile hung on her lips. She wore a black short-sleeved dress, with a necklace across her chest that held a charm the shape of an almond seed. She was beautiful, he thought, probably in her late twenties at the time.

She spoke suddenly, looking at the picture, 'You don't look like your mother.'

She turned back to face him, looking pleased.

'When you see *them*, when you speak to *them*, do you not think about this? I mean your mother and Zakiyya. You don't seem angry enough.' Then, like someone driven to a painful truth, she added, 'Truly, you are not angry like you should be.'

There was accusation and blame in her tone, a deep and wounding blame.

The Visitation Permit that he obtained for his mother came like a miracle after many long months and five attempts to obtain it. Before she was given the permission to see her village, or what remained of it, she had come to the verge of death. The permit struck him with a deep, fated fear and a sense of transgression. He knew the permit would not be sufficient to bring her to the village. It did not authorize her to go inside what they called the Green Line, nor did it include access to Jerusalem, where she wanted to pray. Zakariyya was inside the Green Line, so passage there required a more complex permit.

The whole affair entailed a long period of machinations, an incredible number of documents, certifications, pledged collateral, favours asked from influential friends, and advice from anyone with experience and knowledge.

The issue put him into a confused state, because it seemed to involve a complete reversal of the regular state of things. He now took over the role that his mother had played in all of life's catastrophes. She was the one always looking for a way they might return to the house, she was the one who went beyond the ambition of applying for a mere Visitation Permit, but hoped also Lam al-Shaml—the highest degree among the levels of obtaining permission. The stages of permission progressed through the Permission of Passage, Permission of Visitation, Permission of Commerce, Permission to Visit Relatives, Permission to Work, Airport Permission, Bridge Permission, Prayer Permission, Permission for Treatment—these multiple and subdivided authorizations proliferated to shroud life in what appeared like a 'system', an obscurely engendered, unending chain of lessons and conditions, they formed an arbitrary assembly of accumulating signs that covered this place, yet materialized somehow to become a living, enduring, dominant force that structured the movements and desires of the people.

The 'system' grew in parallel to their lives, as they passed among its dimensions by forced consent.

It was precisely this consent that struck fear in him as he watched the others from his own chosen place, as he saw them wander in the labyrinth of the system with shut eyes and obliging feet. They had been passing through this commotion, seeking their basic needs now for nearly half a century, they could not think of a daily routine of life without it.

He tried with great effort to detach from the 'system', to reduce his daily needs as much as possible to maintain some distance from it. By reducing the demands of his life, he seemed to reduce the submission that life entailed. He had to be more particular about the goods he bought, to constantly ask the grocer the source of his vegetables, cigarettes and coffee. This became a deeply ingrained habit. The only zone of contact that was not in his power to avoid was the Bridge, the border passage that had become his only route to the outside. When his exit procedures had concluded, he would watch the vans pass over the murky green water. He traced the mystic beat of the plodding wheels on the wooden form of the Bridge. That was before they erected the new cement bridge. From that point on, he could only stare at the metal placard recognizing Japan's participation in the construction of the new bridge, thinking back to the old bridge, its brittle body splayed across a bend of the river.

Everything disintegrated when he was within the system. His only thought became his mother's desire, her pressing need for that visit.

Saeed Asks Fatima about the Process

Lam al-Shaml was a pervasive but impossible prize, a ghostly prospect inside every home. It was unclear why this term had been chosen, an ephemeral, dialectal term with no trace of linguistic integrity. But the term preserved its mysterious power to connote the gathering of families that had been split apart for many decades.

Despite everything, this magic sign somehow brought definition to all this absence, signalling the possibility of return of vanished children who had been seated at school desks when the occupation arrived and the troops advanced past their houses. It gave a sign somehow to the children who had never returned from long decades of waiting, and all those who ran in the wrong direction to find cover from the shelling, massacres and aeroplanes; those who had no idea that they were deciding their fate in these instants of terror, who did not know that their location, identity card and future worlds were being determined, or that some quick move or sudden transmission of advice—jump over there, drop down, go to your grandmother's house—would entail all this absence.

The term 'Lam al-Shaml', with all its hopeless promise, had been stripped of context to become an unending chain of procedures, papers, conditions, signatures and stamps, years spent in review lines listening to the other people who waited, who often told their stories in such irritatingly mundane ways.

Fatima, for example, their neighbour in the opposite building, who had been seeking Lam al-Shaml for her husband Saeed for more than twenty years. She kept on waiting in line even after he ended his exiled life by dying *there* to the east of the river. She held to her routine pursuit of reviews, kept on questioning the functionaries concerned with the procedure, checking in on the matter as if nothing had changed, as if Saeed was still there on the other side of the river calling her each night to ask about the process.

None of her companions in line could bring themselves to ask her, or to show any hint of surprise that the matter carried on as before. She went on standing, waiting, asking, as if fulfilling an obligation, holding on to her deeply ingrained routine. Fatima pretended ignorance of Saeed's death, to resist the fact that he would never return. Within the procedure, he remained *present*, within the mass of papers that kept growing and expanding, within an old picture buried in the papers that showed him staring with alarm towards the camera. He was kept alive through the course of the process—his return was still possible. To end or cancel the process would be to pull the breathing tube from the ailing patient's mouth, and she had no desire or the ability to do that.

She was in need, too, of the companions, the skills that she acquired in the long years of review. Her review companions treated her with an attitude of silent collaboration. As long as the matter remained in progress, she would descend from her flat every Wednesday morning to wait for the yellow Ford truck that stopped at the small junction on its way up to al-Amari Refugee Camp, then dropped her near the Connections Office, where she would be joined by the other reviewers to continue the way on foot. He watched her from his window each Wednesday. He watched Abu Ali, the widower, step away from his sweets stand to offer her a piece of carefully wrapped baklava, he heard the repeating pattern of talked exchanged between the two and he knew, as did the whole neighbourhood, that Abu Ali wanted to be closer to her. She alone seemed not to notice the persistent, shy attempts by the man in his fifties.

Very few ever arrived to the finish line of Lam al-Shaml. Their stories, embellished by all the waiters in lines, spread like indications of repeatable miracles, to fortify the stance of those in the lines, nourishing their patience, affirming the steadfastness that was perhaps their final possession.

Hayjar, for example, had been able to get back the dead body of her husband all the way from Columbia, in order to bury him in front of the house. She had plunged steadfastly into a morass of impossible-seeming procedures, first enduring the denials and regulations of the occupation, then faced the objections of Muslim religious men to her proposal to embalm and freeze the body until the procedures of Lam al-Shaml were fulfilled. Even then, when these objections were surpassed, the matter was to come before judges, there was a long court procedure. But she had accomplished it in the end. One could see Hayjar now in her village north of Ramallah, seated with coffee in the morning before his grave, greeting the neighbourhood women and watching schoolchildren descend the valley through lines of olive trees towards the paved road on their way to school. She seemed to be speaking familiar words to her husband, happy and calm, transformed beyond the woman who had plunged into long, enduring battle, who had carried in her heart the coffin of her deceased husband. Now she could sit as if everything she was born for was accomplish, as if the grave was a promise fulfilled.

Failure of the Old Man's Second Attempt

The old man failed for a second time. The machine gate went back to its anxious drone. With intense apology, the man looked to the Arab worker, the exasperated woman soldier behind the glass, and the long line that kept growing behind the yellow line. Men, women and children all stared at him, as if coaxing him to jump from a perilous ledge. He strained to gather his will. He had taken off his overcoat and looked much thinner now in front of the gateway.

He now started to imagine the man as his uncle, Mahmoud, who had passed away in the town of Rusifa, north of Amman, years earlier, having never obtained the Visitation Permit he had hoped for. He had always had a vague feeling that he resembled Uncle Mahmoud more than he did the rest of the family. He had kept this feeling like a small secret that only amplified when he visited him at his house on the mountain north of town.

It was this old man's leanness, his tall, bent stature, that triggered him to see his uncle now standing in front of the machine, unable to pass to the other side.

Mahmoud had been in his mind when he made his first visit to Zakariyya, especially when he entered the tomb. Inside it, he had tried to re-create the angles in the photograph of the low-reaching arches of the roof, the window edge, and the tree shadows that spread like smeared coal on the white lime walls. But it was Mahmoud's presence that touched him in the movements of the cold inner air, whispering things that he could not quite make out. It was the unhurried voice of his dead uncle, who had told him about the brides of the jinn he once saw in this tomb between sleep and waking, the bodies of the jinn that passed in ranks between the arches, the rattle of necklaces, the clicking of bangles, the dresses rustling in invisible celebrations.

He had been unable in Zakariyya to summon his father, who appeared only later, in connection to the scene of the railway station, descending from the train and rising through the forest towards the village.

The village itself, splayed in front of its short minaret, which had been stripped of its crescent by one of *them*, seemed blind and crucified, incapable of breath. But his uncle's presence had encircled him when he reached the village tomb, amplifying his feeling of their shared resemblance.

She leant back in her seat. It seemed that she might pose some question, or rise from the glass box where he had always seen her. She took his passport through the small aperture.

'You travel often,' she said in broken Arabic that reminded him of Hind's soldier.

'For work,' he said in English.

He felt his hands sweating on the cover of the book he was carrying, and placed it onto the ledge of the glass checkpoint. She looked around in the narrow glass box as if assessing its dimensions, then looked back at him. It was again this look that asserted some need to speak. She began flipping pages of the passport, he could sense the effort she was spending searching for her next question. He considered if he could offer some bridge or avenue to keep going with her talk. Beads of sweat were visible on her chest. She was in her thirties, he thought. They usually send anxious, sullen adolescent girls here, but this one seemed different. He tried arduously to set her apart, to detach her from her resemblance to *them*. If she could depart that group, he could continue to talk with her, only at some remove where she could differ just slightly, enough for him to perceive her in some other way. But he knew perfectly well this was some delusion.

'Do you speak Hebrew?' she asked in English.

'No.'

He felt undeniable relief. In a third language, a feeling came like arrival to some calm place of shadow, a neutral, chilled region that held their existence and strangeness together.

She stamped the pass and went on flipping the pages, as if noticing every stamp and travel visa. Then she returned it to him through the window.

'Will you be over there long?'

Her voice pierced him. She seemed to be exacting some privileged right to question him, to be asserting some unsolicited entitlement that arose merely through their proximity.

'I don't understand.'

'Will you be over there long this time?'

As her gaze lingered into his eyes, he saw she was afraid. Her voice was less sure this time.

'No.'

He was also afraid. He added,

'I don't know.'

Blind Body Beyond the Window

Hind said, 'The last night I was unable to sleep. The idea of going back *there* had gathered. I couldn't keep things in order any more, or be content about how things are. Everything seemed like an overwhelming betrayal, everything, everything I knew, sensed or saw, the betrayal of exile, isolating me, removing me from anything that could happen from now on. I sat in front of the window and knew that I would not come back here. The window looked far into the distance, over the orange and lemon orchards that stretch towards Tyre along the coast. The darkness of the vineyard was thick in front of me and somewhere in this darkness people were celebrating. A group was singing and dancing, there were voices of men, extending and spreading like gifts being passed back and forth rapidly, exciting the air in front of the window. No doubt there was a dancer, probably a woman. One could hear this in the freedom of the male voices. From where I was, I imagined her body's movement as it turned inside the circle. I centred on the rushes of feeling in the male voices. I could sense the strands of their desire advance and the harshness as it left their bodies. I tried to sense the dancer, to imagine her power and fear, her isolation in the confining circle of men that collapsed around her, their clapping hands extended in front of them as if carving passages in the air for their fast breath to reach and flood her body.

'I had to close my eyes to advance through the window, into the darkness. I met the heavy scents that diffused in the sea air, the scents of the vineyards at night as they filled with the sounds of the bodies of men. The ordered blows of their feet went in rhythm to the tilting of their connected shoulders, the rhythm merging with the scent of their sweat. I watched the body become encircled and captured by the fast inward warping of the circling dancers. That was all it was. The scent of the vineyards, the sweltering, damp air that crept through the openings of their shirts like an impassioned, unrelenting caress. The caressing grew wider and more certain as she circled, as she became wet, as she was probed and uncovered, the air diffused and scampered to its aims, refreshing, glancing, expanding like a hurried excuse, satisfying, sighing, pulling, lapping, drinking, mocking, coming forward from all directions towards this central point in the darkness, the small body that was being taken somewhere beyond the window.'

He could not know if this is exactly what she said, or if he had made additions to what she said, sitting in her usual leather rocking chair like a recoiled panther ready to pounce, pushing her feet forward as she went on speaking.

'I was young when it happened,' Hind continued. 'It was another wedding. We lived in a camp on the east bank of the Jordan River, a hastily built camp that had accumulated on that salty part of land. The inhabitants tried to farm the land, to extract the salt from the soil and cultivate it under a burning sun, and to keep poisonous snakes and malaria mosquitoes away from their children. It was the wedding party of one of the notables, the owner of a shop in the middle of the market. Shakir—that was the name of the father—provided everything to the farmers, from tea to chemical fertilizer, to boxes of cheap make-up for flirtatious women and brides. Shakir's area was on the edge of the camp towards the fields. It was a wide enclosure, and in its centre was a drainage pit covered over with cement—it looked like a theatre stage lain on top of the ground. Two large benches of woven reeds were placed on top of it for the bride and groom, and behind them was a wreath woven from palm branches. Chairs were placed on the platform over the pit, and a straw umbrella for the people of greatest importance—the camp manager, the principal of the school, the head of the guard post and the relatives of the bride and groom.

'Before evening prayer, the camp in its entirety crept towards Shakir's enclosure. Women towed their children and boys ran through alleys like jumping grasshoppers. Young men and women came forward in their decorations, eager to show their talents for dancing and singing, alongside farming men and Bedouins who came down from the mountain to tie their donkeys at the entrances of the space.

'The rumoured arrival of Dallal the Dancer with her troupe had built up to a true fever in the camp's imagination. She was coming to herald the marriage.

'It was something like a strange carnival. Dallal, the full woman, with her sharp tongue and famous dance costume, had become a myth enflaming the imagination of the men in the camp. Some even followed her from wedding to wedding along the banks of the river, embellishing her with anything that their imaginations and desires permitted. She had become like a mermaid that emerged directly from the *1,001 Nights*.

'A string of electric lights had been stretched over the space, tied to two wooden poles on the two sides, so that light spilt mainly onto the bride and groom, the dancer and the most prominent invitees. Somewhere a dabka circle was being improvised, and at a remove from the light, where the women were gathered, tuneless singing, loud voices, and the shouts of children rose out of the darkness. Then everything fell silent. When Dallal entered, her legendary costume reflected all the light. The cheap hanging decorations started to flicker within it, enrapturing the camp. The costume showed her full legs, parts of her back and chest, and moments of her hot-pink bra, enough to confirm what many knew of her body and meet the flood of rumours that had proceeded this moment. Now she stood in the middle of the enclosure, among the bride, groom and the invited guests, as a firm, indisputable truth.

'She was a beautiful woman. Her body was fulsome, yet taut and chiselled. Her smile was brazen, and somewhat broken.

'According to those who knew, she was a refugee from one of the cities on the coast, Jaffa it was said, and she lived now in Jericho and was unmarried. At a sign from her hand, her troupe entered the circle. An oud player, a drummer, an arghul player and a singer formed a row behind her. Seats now arrived for the group to sit at the feet of the bride and groom. Only the arghul player remained standing.

'Suddenly the sound of the arghul rose. It was unfathomable—I have heard nothing like it, to this day. The musician was a short man with dark skin, and he played his cane instrument as if it were the flute that was blowing into his body. He himself seemed to be the only person showing no interest whatsoever in whatever occurred around him, lost in his work from the moment he started. He looked forward with bulging eyes, beyond the body of Dallal, towards the heads of those seated, and off into the darkness. The swift manipulations of his fingers embellished the long, rising opening melody, filling the space with some secret language. His face could never be forgotten.

'The bodies started to push together into the space, just as the sound of the arghul gave way to the oud and drums. Without prelude, Dallal leapt to the middle of the circle, shaking the necklaces that enveloped her. Her body began to bend and writhe exquisitely, her breasts surged under her pink bra that seemed to push her backwards. Only the surge of her backside could restore the balance of her full and coherent body as, somewhere in this movement, her broken smile lingered.

'Excited boys arrived to the enclosure, as if executing some earlier agreement, pressing themselves into a compact circle that surrounded Dallal to block the view of the seated guests. The light spilling from the bulbs strung overhead reached all of them. Dallal's face began to signal some cavernous satisfaction as the circle narrowed around her, as bodies of men weaved together, closing the space inside the shrinking, hot, noisy circle. The sound of the arghul swelled and rose again like an enormous uncoiling snake. Dallal, in the centre of the circle, moved on her bare feet, swaying her torso in widening half-circles, her eyes flashing as the circlets around her chest and backside glimmered. Her full, uncovered body shone with beads of sweat. The breathing and panting of the men hissed their terrifying, dominating collective desire. The beating of their feet on the cement floor grew louder, and now their faces and eyes disappeared. They became only the panting of their breath and the tendons that stretched from their necks to their shoulders.

'But then it started, as a hidden roar. There was a high-pitched crack, and the confused shouting. The cement covering of the drainage pit had broken, from the centre outward. A total collapse followed. First the sound of the arghul, then the oud, then the rhythm, all fell into the pit. Dallal, the arghul player, the oud player, the drummer and the singer, who had not yet started singing, then the show-bench on which the bride and groom were seated, the circle of dancers, the guests on the front chairs, the umbrella, the remainder of the circle and some children who had been crawling among them, they all fell into the pit. Dust rose from below, and a dreadful, putrid smell emerged to fill the place. Screams came now from inside the wastewater of the drainage pit. Dallal's voice could be made out, making foul curses against everything, even the bride and groom, the camp and her profession.

'The camp stayed awake all night until morning, engaged in the rescue operation. There was extreme embarrassment and agonizing pain, as they emerged, one by one, swamped in the foulness of the pit. Each person was rolled into a blanket, to be dried under the eyes of the camp, amid the comments of those who had been safe from the event and the laughter of women and children.

'The line of electric lights was still fixed, dealing the light below, redoubling the tragic dimension of the scene.'

He wished her story had ended before the fateful collapse. It shattered the image of the dancer he had crafted in his imagination with the help of a rare article by Edward Said about Taheyya Kariokka, the famous Arab dancer of the twentieth century. Said had gone to her house to interview her, to produce a kind of tribute to his early youth in Egypt, recalling the days of the early Fifties when Taheyya was at the peak of her brilliance. He was mesmerized by her smile, which he had called 'a fixed smile in an overturned world'.

But she told the story to its saddening end. Dallal's fate could no longer be tied into Said's illumination of Taheyya.

First Appearance of Rivka, the Train and
the Station Guard in Mother's Story

His mother could not understand what exactly prevented her from going to Zakariyya or from praying
in Jerusalem. She was consumed by the idea that she
held 'permission', and the situation could not really
be explained to her. Every attempt at clarification
was met with,

'But they gave us permission to visit!'

It was impossible to explain to her the stages and
degrees of permission, their various efficacies and the
endless pathways of the 'system'. She continued to
make silent, tormenting signals in his direction as
they sat on the balcony during the first days after his
arrival in Ramallah. A portal seemed to have been
wrenched open in her memory, and it could never
be shut again.

Now she brought forth the village, as if she had returned there, as if she was trying to make sure of their existence, that they were there, that Zakariyya truly existed. She brought forward all the persons on the eve of the migration, their ages, forms, qualities, nicknames, enmities, jealousies and passions, all the stories that stood unfinished, propped up endlessly against their heroes. She treated her narrative, with all its furnishings, as if she were handling a pledge that she had held in her heart, whose time had come to be redeemed to its owner.

They sat there, away from war and terror, free of all disquieting knowledge, within small, abbreviated stories, inside snapshots of windows, stairs and attics, like the affectionate and amused story of the lover who brought bottles of perfume from Jaffa to douse the tracks of his beloved. He had listened to this story many times. It was his favourite one. He had even met the man once in one of the camps in Jordan, and he could remember him as an old and silent man. It was perhaps this that made him love the man so much in that vivid and precisely drawn scene. He imagined the traces of the woman's bare feet on the dirt path. Her name was Aisha, he thought. He

watched the lover following her trail, as Aisha
focussed on her feet, choosing the softest places on
the path so that he could easily locate her tracks.
From his seat on the balcony in Ramallah, he followed the smell of the perfume to the threshold of
her house.

It was then that the proposal of his American
friend, the woman journalist, appeared like some
long-awaited miracle. She said, 'I will bring her there
in my car. It won't raise any doubts for them.'

'Don't forget,' she added, 'I am an American, and
a journalist. They will be cautious.'

He thought of his mother's kerchief and the veil
that she waved. He could not bear the thought of
her being taken down from the car and inspected,
the probing implications of the questions, then her
being loaded onto the Bridge and returned to Jordan
on the pretext that she was violating the specifica-
tions of the Permission.

But the journalist went on with her proposal.
She even turned to his mother and demonstrated her
offer meticulously, using hand gestures, facial expressions and three Arabic words, and then the full throt-
tle of her English language. She bowed down until

she almost touched the ground, almost down on her knees. His mother stared at her for a moment, then she asked him,

'Is this woman Jewish?'

'She is not from here, Hajja, she is American.'

'But she is Jewish.'

'Jewish American, Hajja. She is not Israeli.'

'I had a Jewish Palestinian friend, she was from Artouf. Her name was Rivka. I don't know what happened to her after the migration.'

His mother still used the word 'migration', not catastrophe.

'She says that she will take you to Zakariyya in her car.'

She went on, paying no attention to his remark or to the journalist sitting on the ground moving her eyes between them.

'Rivka came down from Artouf and crossed the forest towards the railway station. I told you, there is a railway track that crosses the valley, and there is a small station. There was a guard from Jerusalem, a man who was quite old, without wife or children, who lived in the station and never left, and he was

nice to everyone. When it rained, he would bring us
into his room, Rivka and me, so that we wouldn't
get wet. We sat behind the window and watched the
train pass while rain fell on the huge eucalyptus trees,
and we boiled tea in an old zinc pitcher. He put three
lumps of sugar for each of us. She and I, Rivka and
I, we used to meet at the station. She came on foot
to wait for her mother. I came with the horse, Saleh,
and waited for your uncle, then later your father. I
always watched the trains. I loved watching the trains.
I have not seen a train since the migration. She was
around my age, brown and thin with thick eyebrows
and a braid that reached her shoulder. We sat, like
I told you, under an old eucalyptus tree, enjoying
ourselves and carving our names in the tree trunk,
waiting for the train. We listened to its whistle as it
stopped at the bends of the wadi on the way from
Jerusalem. Before the final turn, the guard would put
on his cap and go to stand on the platform to greet
the train. At the beginning we just sat there, but later
we started to chat. After her mother got off the train,
she asked her, "Is this your friend?"

Rivka said yes.

But we were not friends yet.

Her mother, who worked as a nurse in Jerusalem, fetched two little candies from her bag, and handed them to me.'

His mother continued her outpouring. The two of them, he and the journalist, just stared into the story. The many minor details engulfed the story and its characters: the grassy sides of the wadi, the reeds and pine trees declining against the bluff, ancient eucalyptus trees, the train whistle, the colours of the train carriages, the flashing metal buckle on the handbag of the nurse coming from Jerusalem, the coloured paper wrapped around the candy, the guard's cap, the smell of tea and the thin, brown Jewish girl. The shutters of a window that had been locked for fifty years had had been flung open, it seemed, and the Jewish girl entered, with her Arab face, brown eyes and uncovered hair. It were as if a stream, long confined, had found a passage to flow.

It reminded him of the poem 'When He Goes Away' by Mahmoud Darwish. In the poem, the daughter of the enemy resembles Rivka. There's also a horse snorting in memory, prodded by over-flying aeroplanes—or something like that. He could not imagine Rivka without recalling the poem.

The enemy sips tea in our hut,
He has a horse in the smoke
and a girl with thick eyebrows and brown eyes,
her air filled with song on her shoulders.
Her picture is with him
when he comes to ask for tea.
He does not tell of her errands in the night
or the horse left on the hill by song.

In our hut the enemy relieves himself
of his rifle
and leans on my grandfather's chair.
He eats our bread
and dozes like a guest
on the wicker chair,
or strokes the fur of our cat.
He says not to blame the victim.
We ask him, who is she?
Blood, he says,
that the night has not dried.

His jacket buttons shine as he leaves.
Good evening, please greet
our well and the fig groves,
walk light on our shaded barley fields,
and say hello to our cypresses.

Please, do not forget
the doorway to our house
left open in the night, do not forget
the horse's fear of the aeroplane.
Greet us, over there, if there is time.

He rearranged the furnishings: the horse and its fear of aeroplanes was exchanged for anxiety about the train whistle; the enemy, the father, was exchanged easily for the mother nurse coming from Jerusalem; Rivka, the daughter of the enemy, replaced Rita, the white woman soldier in several of Darwish's poems, with her distinct voice and tenor, and her vividly delineated features. Rivka, in contrast, was a faint, deep voice that left ripples in the air. The place where she emitted her qualities was beyond Rita, in a place covered by grey sky, where a long winter was pouring down, and a pine forest was leaning into the bluff. There, he watched Rivka descend to the railway station, then touch the shoulders of his mother who had arrived first.

Will You Be Gone Long This Time?

He passed by the second woman soldier who checked over the stamps, then the third soldier who reviewed them again. Then he crossed the checkpoint that led to the exit door. A tall, young man stood there beside the bus that would transport them to the Jordanian side. He was lighting a cigarette and staring towards the exit, waiting for his friend who had disappeared behind one of the doors. He looked lost, and the movements of his hands and eyes suggested some confusion, almost as if to voice some obscure apology. He approached the young man and stood next to him, to give him a chance to fulfil his palpable need to speak. But the confused boy did nothing, only kept his painful watch on the exit. Having given up the idea of speaking with the young man, he smoked cigarettes to pass the last few minutes before departure, looking through the windows into the depth of the hall.

The old man was loosening his belt with an exhausted and hopeless look, staring through the machine gate with a feeling of total submission next to a jumbled pile of belongings.

Maybe he was on his way to visit a son or grandson, he thought. He did not seem to be going for medical treatment, and there were no travelling companions to help him through. The old man seemed to have exerted great effort in choosing his clothes, he thought. He wore a black-checked keffiyeh with long fringes, clearly of a noble source, and a grey qunbaz robe with broad dark stripes. He wanted to keep looking at him, but the bus driver had climbed up to his seat and flicked away the rest of his cigarette, and was now preparing to leave.

The fat man was in a seat close to the door, and the family had settled into three seats by a window, with Yusuf now in his mother's lap, trying to pull at the curtains on the window. The tall, young man kept standing at his spot. He chose a seat at the back of stationary bus. Then he found himself recalling her frightened voice.

'Will you be gone long this time?'

His life was filled with abrupt signals like this, he thought. Early indications, stories that almost never finish but transform over time into mild regrets laced by curiosity and the repetition of memory. Faces filing into a line, lit by the past, spontaneously filled by thirst. His hobby, his private game through the long arch of the years, was to attempt to complete the signs, to dis-assemble them and build new stories around them. But this often brought him confused, contradictory sensations, when everything became cloudy and obscurely trodden. A young woman seated at the back of a yellow school bus was still alive, and she looked at him now, some forty years later, with still-dark eyes behind a bus window, as he paused on a street corner before some dark alley. He didn't know how this happened, or if they had both agreed to it.

And there was the posture of the young woman, pale and white, on the second-floor balcony of her house, as he sat in darkness keeping watch on her sleep, as if positioned on some balcony in her dream. She was half Circassian, he remembered. It all looked like a scene from a silent love story in black and white. The girl still had this power to remain, over so many years, leaning on the balcony.

Years later, by some strange accident, the two of them met in a room lit by an old chandelier, enclosed by thick curtains and the smell of damp carpets and moth balls. They spoke not a single word. She reached her hand out to him, holding a picture that she had taken from her handbag. It showed a boy beside a girl who greatly resembled her. She seemed to have left her reclining position on the balcony just to show him the photo. Then she went back. He handed the picture to her. Speech would have been a betrayal of the silent story that existed between them. For a moment, he was baffled that the two of them could be visiting the house together. Clearly, none of this could be real. None of this should be seeded with any speech, no questions or curiosity. They had to return to where their story was real.

He thought again of the boredom of the woman soldier, magnified by the glass partition at the checkpoint, a deep ennui that pervaded her freckles and gave her a perplexed look.

Maybe she was Russian, he thought. He could recall many women like her from his visits to

Moscow before the collapse of the Soviet Union. Olga especially, the young poet who worked in the government peace agency, whom he had met only once, on the evening of the collapse. Groups of dissenters were taking to the city streets, as the two of them snuck out the back door of the hotel into the street to join the shouting crowds. In this chaos they had to find her car, which she had parked somewhere on the side streets beside the hotel. Before they reached the pavement, they had to pierce the rows of confused security men. Scared and upset, Olga had suddenly seized his hand as they raced through the angry crowds.

Back at the hotel at five that morning, she did not come up to the room as they had planned. She was troubled, but she kissed him with force. He tried to shrug off the sudden sense of guilt that overcame him, in front of the hotel entrance, perhaps at the thought that he would leave her behind in the crowd thronging the city streets. The memory of the night still tormented him, especially her bravery as she called out in Russian holding on to his hand. The Russians were going to rearrange their house, as it happens every hundred years, and the world watched on, as it happens every hundred years, anxious and holding its breath. He said, finally, 'I will come back in November.'

He had not intended to do that, and he did not know why he said it. But he repeated the promise as she put her hand to his lips.

Two hours later, he travelled back home. He never learnt what happened to the poet. He did not return in November. He often found himself recalling that journey and the final night. Even now, with some effort, he could remember the short poem that she wrote for him, which was translated by a friend who had studied in Moscow. Despite all the mistakes that pervaded that engineering student's translation, it still conveyed the idea of loss. He had been convinced that she had disappeared forever in those discontented crowds, and that this was what she had wanted. He watched her raise her fist, shouting in Russian but not losing his hand at her back, as he followed, stunned by the bodies that crowded against him, by the shattered cars, statues and park fences that surrounded them along their way. He knew nothing about the Russians that surrounded him, he only knew that it was impossible for them to be returned to their houses. The security men, staring at the protestors, looked at their banners and heard their chants, like witnesses to a miracle. In shocking instants, some of the security men joined in with the hordes, as if leaping from a cliff into the waters that flooded through a deep abyss.

He was certain that night that Olga, timid and beautiful, was headed to her family home. He knew she had abandoned her life as it had been, that she had to accept that she would leave behind her dreams to walk barefoot on the tips of her toes.

He thought of Olga, also, when he read the letters between Rilke and the Russian poet Marina Tsvetaeva. It was years after the night of demonstrations in Moscow, as he was reading anything that might help him to enter the German poet's world. Through the lens of Marina's miserable fate, he came to see Rilke as an elderly, confused stage performer. Marina was alive and effusive, with a dark, flooding anger that coursed through her chaotic longing. There was anger and intractability in the overlapping of poetry and description that filled her letters, as if she were setting out to annihilate her own energy for writing, to dissipate it by bringing it to extremes.

She seemed to have some inescapable, idealist faith in the act of writing, a faith that erased the borders between poetry and letter writing.

Rilke was more guarded and protective of his faculties. For him, a letter was a letter, nothing more or less—for him, it was just a letter to a young and beautiful woman who seemed attractive in his few pictures of her. There was some hidden motivation in his writing, perhaps his affection for Russia and his obscure desire to be connected to it, and it was just a stroke of luck that the young, effusive woman who sent him burning letters was Russian, and living in exile.

He could bring back only a few of the lines of the poem that Olga had dedicated to him ten years earlier, but from these few lines he could retrieve the idea of assent, in all its power, from the writing.

I lift my cup
to an endless journey,
to your new road
and new betrayal.
I do not envy
whoever waits for you eagerly.
I drink in silence,

and I am not your happiness.
Let her wait
while we finish our dinner.
The sun at noon
is within everyone's reach,
and I do not live in the light.
But in the evening
maybe I
dream a soft glow.
I will not be your sun,
but at night's dark hour
I might be your candle.

Then he thought, too, of the cleaner woman at
the hotel. Beginning with the first night of his stay,
she had asked him strange questions which he did
not quite understand, but she carried on relentlessly.
On the sixth day, he asked Olga to translate, which
only made him feel more alone, isolated and
aggrieved. The cleaning woman wanted to know if
he was Palestinian, and if he knew of Muhammad.
Muhammad, who had been there for seven years, had
married her daughter Zouia, and lived with her like
her son. He was good and kind and she now had a
grandson, five years old, who looked exactly like him.

A year earlier, Muhammad had returned to visit his family, then all word of him stopped. The woman worried for Muhammad, in the effusive, maternal way that only a Russian woman from the countryside can perfect. She was afraid, also, of what was happening in the streets. The factory where Zouia worked had closed, and Kareem, who looked like his father, asked about him constantly and hung pictures of him on the walls of their flat. She was afraid now that she would lose her position in the hotel amid the chaos.

He could only say that he would ask about Muhammad. He could not bring himself to tell her that he lived in another country, and that he could not even go *there*, where it would be possible to ask about Muhammad. To seed just a small bit of hope in her heart, he asked for Muhammad's full name. 'Muhammad Abd al-Kareem,' she replied. He saw that the man had named his son after his father. Olga translated for him, patiently, with affection. She also knew that he could not help the Russian woman, and she saw the whole affair as absurd and tragic, as she confessed later.

The stories all felt missing and incomplete from where he stood now, at the tomb behind the monastery, or in the coffee shop of the Moroccan woman. Hind, too, seemed like a missing story. Their return seemed like a missing return. The place had turned out to be missing, the dreams and appointments all unfulfilled. The war was missing, like Olga's poem, like the waters that run in Wadi Qelt, like the sea and the river. Things do not arrive. His life seemed to inflect into isolation, a series of incomplete returns, all built on a single return that was never accomplished, pressing its incompletion against everything. He had been pursued by a void which was his inescapable destination. From where he stood now, he knew things would not be complete without her.

Kattan, Habibi, Kertész, al-Qisi

He could have kept sifting through those signs, had
he not suddenly remembered that he left his book on
the ledge in the checkpoint. *Farewell, Babylon* by
Naïm Kattan, a book in which Kattan, a Jewish Iraqi
living in Canada, wrote about his early life in Baghdad
in the Forties, then his emigration to Canada. It was
the safest way for him to speak to *them,* to borrow
them in books, where he could hold their hands,
place his hands on their shoulders and walk with
them, exchanging long and painful conversations. He
was trying this now with Naïm Kattan. From the first
page, a thread pulled him towards the young Jewish
man who sat in the salon of his house in a Baghdad
neighbourhood of the early Forties. In some ways,
the life story was very familiar. The hesitant boy came
from somewhere close to him, somewhere closer
than the book or the mere facts of his life.

Kattan spoke about some 'agreement', a treaty of coexistence that had continued for more than thirteen centuries but which, according to Kattan, reached a breaking point during the time that his life story occurred. The agreement, he said, was now breaking apart and dissolving. Somehow, he found this unconvincing. This perplexed, ambivalent Jewish youth, so desperately desirous to get out of the city and the agreement, to go beyond his house, language and dialect, still held some innocence that existed beyond this deceptive narrative.

A different agreement seemed to emerge between himself and the young man, at a remove from the interferences of Kattan who tried with great effort, and at every instant, to magnify his own position and the ideas of the young Jew. He attended to the gaps that Kattan had been unable to erase or hide, gaps that crept out, despite the studied narrative, in longing and description, and in the Jewish boy's attempts to write in Arabic. For his part, he tried to befriend the young man through his ardent understanding of the boy's fear to remain here or venture out, his unwillingness to give up the deep feelings of bitterness, loss and deprivation that had grown somehow into a sense of betrayal. At the same time, Kattan, from his residence in Canada, cast reasons, expedients and doubts onto the boy, attempting to amplify his fear of flight and to equate his 'exile' in Baghdad with his Canadian 'exile'.

The transformation of all of that into an 'agreement' of coexistence, after cleansing anything that might attest to the idea of a homeland, the seeding of the signs of exile and then the tireless search for a breach of that 'agreement', all this enabled Kattan to manufacture his personal holocaust, to endorse his own betrayal and validate the cargo of 'rights' and justifications that he took away with him.

Kattan's story displayed a longing not for place as much as for narrative. He showed a deep confidence, unintended and submerged, in his new place and his new language. Yet, he felt that a partnership took form between them, between him and Kattan, somewhere within the revolutions of memory. It was a partnership in confusion, accomplished by the force of his exclusion from the place of remembrance, and by the real, physical threats that engulfed him, regardless of the relative degree of severity. There had been constrictions of his breath, movement and language, until he had reached Canada and acquired the French language, where his exile became complete, where his rooms and halls were furnished with the belongings he held in his banishment, fitted to the exertions and desires of exile itself. This way, his exile reached its most extreme potential. It was transformed into homeland.

His partnership with Kattan ended before he reached that point, before he had cleansed his memories of the longing that grows in details, like garden plants, to translate into the dream of return.

Kattan accomplished the task that he began in the first half of the last century. He purified his story, through a single act of assassination, metaphorical and cruel, against his first place. This was what *he* was not able, and never willing, to do. His difference with Kattan began here, in that he built his memories on an idea of return, a fated and ineluctable salvation, while Kattan formed his narrative on an idea of departure. His departure from Baghdad seemed to be the point and purpose of his redemption. No return occurred anywhere in that story, which was structured around the idea of diaspora, but which stayed clear of the final chapter of that mythology, the figuring of a 'promised land'. It was asserted that the Lord had chosen for him his diaspora, but he himself took up the role of the Lord in bringing about the perfection of his new exile, which then became his personal 'promised land'.

For the purpose of comparison, or perhaps to put a decisive end to Kattan's pretexts, or perhaps to comfort the young Jewish man who sat in coffee shops in Baghdad in the Forties conversing with young Jews and Arabs, he approached the boy and put his hand on his shoulder, and he pointed him towards Haifa, where another boy was wandering. Emile Habibi went among the groups of Palestinians and Jews in the city, trying to protect the Arab houses left behind by terrified families as war erupted in the streets. They were trying to protect the houses from being taken over by the emigrating Jews who streamed behind the army, carrying bags and belongings.

Naïm Kattan, from his place of settlement in Canada, had tried to justify the young man's idea of emigration, to push him towards it by transforming it into an act of resistance or refuge or, at the very least, a move from a humiliating agreement into another agreement that might achieve a shift from captivity to voluntary migration. But Emile Habibi had returned to his house, exhausted, and now sat in the salon in a faint light. He looked into the eyes of a Jewish immigrant who had arrived and placed his bags on the chair in the entryway, who now walked through the space of a house that he intended to occupy. 'We did not exchange a single word,' Emile said. 'I just looked into his eyes, and he looked at mine. Then at midnight, he rose and left the house.'

> I had to return to the house. The immigrant's presence in my home was an absurd summation of everything that was happening in Palestine, and all that is still happening: to return from death to save your house and the family pictures on the wall, to preserve your books and the flower vases on the balconies.

Emile asked to be buried in Haifa, with the words 'The remainer in Haifa' on his gravestone. That is how his return was accomplished.

That return was nothing like the return of Saeed Abi al-Nahas the Pessoptimist who was saved from death at the hands of the Jewish troops by a stroke of luck on the road when, as he crept back into his house, a donkey passed between him and the troops as they fired at him.

'The donkey saved me. I owe my life to that donkey.' His father, however, had not been lucky enough to find a donkey.

This then led him to the return of the young Imre Kertész to the threshold of the house that he had left behind, with the assurance that the Permission that he held would allow him to venture safely outside the ghetto and the city. But then there had been those small shifts of fate, and everything that had occurred in the morning at the checkpoint that then led him into the groups of Hungarian Jews bound for Auschwitz, before it became Auschwitz, then Buchenwald, before it became Buchenwald. He wanted to get back to his house, and there had been no 'agreement', no place beyond the residence, no other language. Even the idea of hatred that he held onto so tightly, a hatred that enveloped everything— it, too, disintegrated when he saw the shocking glimmer of the surface water of the Danube on his return. The river marked the way to the house, it indicated his way back, with all that he could carry, having left behind or forgotten nothing. But there was no new beginning. From this moment on, he would remain merely the result of all this, the farewell as his father went to the work camp, which was more like an implicit funeral, the permission to pass, the permission to work, the moment when water poured from the sprinklers instead of gas through some second shift of fate. He had now become all of this, as he rushed in a striped coat through groups of Hungarians towards the house. Behind him was the hand of the Polish Jewish nurse Bitka who had altered his fate decisively by pushing another Jew into the gas showers. The moment had been the terrifying crystallization of his march towards Auschwitz and then the wage factory in Buchenwald. Inside a lit and heated clinic room, the horrific cremation machine was crushing four souls, having crushed four bodies, and the small murder procession moved on from the killing machine to outside the clinic room. The final death sentence was given by a nurse's signal and the silent indifference of the doctor. Bitka's sign was a stretcher for corpses, floating in the air at the level of a man's knee, roaming the sleeping quarters, huts and passages, passing under the yellow searchlights and into the gas showers in the bathrooms. It was like a deep, ravenous pit that could never be filled, leaving hills of corpses, remains of clothes, smuggled necessities and rainwater. Bitka answered the doctor's question with her gesture, controlling the cries of despair that preceded the arrival of the messiah.

He followed the arriving young man, as he followed Naïm Kattan in the Muslim neighbourhoods of Baghdad. He wanted to accompany him to the house where he grew up, the one he had left that morning in Budapest—and no other house. The door that had locked behind him, and no other door. For him to push open that door with his gaunt shoulder, and to look with craving eyes and unflinching hatred into the eyes of the person that had taken over his rooms and memories, just as Emile Habibi stared into the eyes of the occupier on the night of the fall of Haifa, and as he stared now from his grave overlooking the city.

He worried that he would not find the house, or that he would find someone else entirely, that he would open the door to find an astonished person, startled at the young man with jealous eyes and a striped coat, which indicated so clearly where he came from, someone terrified by the young man's memories, terrified by his hatred, terrified that he had not died but had instead returned.

In some unintentional and repetitious way, this took him to the return of Muhammad al-Qaysi, to the house where his mother Hamda al-Bik had found refuge when she was displaced from her village. It was not a complete house, according to Muhammad, who was called 'the wandering poet' because of his three decades of vagrancy between exiles. Rather, through her hard work in the long years of widowhood, she had been able to turn a three-person tent into a tin hut, then, before her second displacement, she had added a cement roof, a door and a narrow courtyard. All of which took her a long time. When she finally locked the door behind her for the first time, she discovered that it was very late. She noted the darkness, and felt the wrinkles under her eyes. In the faint light, she looked at her cracked hands.

The house was located in Jalzoun Refugee Camp next to Ramallah to the north, built on land belonging to a neighbouring Christian village. Israeli settlements were erected in front of the camp after the second war, on land confiscated from the same group of villages. The scene was both absurd and completely deliberate: the Christian village with its church tower, the apricot vineyards that spread through the wadi up to the edges of the camp, and the large school building at the camp entrance, built by a United Nations agency. From classrooms on the second and third floors, the students could see the settlers walking the streets of the settlement with their weapons, over barbed-wire fences and watch-towers on either side.

He had no intention or goal other than to see the house, to confirm his childhood, and to remember his mother, whom he had buried, in her second exile, on a hill covered in phosphate dust in Rusifa, in Jordan.

During the absence, some neighbours had divided up the house, making free use of its areas, and had added a room on the roof and a water closet at the end of the narrow courtyard.

A man, his wife and three children. Two boys and a girl. They lined up in front of me as if they were awaiting a death sentence or posing for a family picture—an old-fashioned shot in black and white. They seemed scared.

The man was silent, meek and shocked, but the wife seemed more coherent. The children's fear was mixed also with curiosity, as they stared at the man in his fifties with long white hair and a black backpack, who had appeared, unannounced, on the threshold of the house like a vague, unrealized threat.

I could not continue. The group defeated me completely. I took two steps back from the doorway, and I continued no further. They were gathered like an immovable rampart in front of my mother's room. They had changed the colour of the door, added a room on the roof, and what looked like a bathroom at the end of the courtyard. I said to the man, attempting to smile to dispel my worry:

I just came for a visit.

The woman continued with a confused and stubborn apology.

It was abandoned, we did not think that you would return . . . we have nowhere to go . . .

I interrupted her, thinking of my mother Hamda al-Bik, and her poor grave on that hill in Rusifa.

You are right. We did not come back.

Exile pounded the souls of all of them—myself, the family, and the long misery of Hamda al-Bik.

As I turned to leave, the man jumped. He had remained meek and silent until now, but now he locked the door behind me with force. He was just behind the door. He, his wife, his two sons and daughter, were all behind the door now, as I started down the narrow passageway, careful not to fall into the open sewage canal or to collide with the heads of the boys and girls that spouted out of the doors on the sides of the canal. He was still afraid, I thought, the meek, silent man. It was as if I had caused all the trouble, by appearing in front of them like a ghost of someone they thought they had buried, simply because I wanted to remember. I had acted almost like some confused tourist in front of those pairs of eyes, especially the curious eyes of the weary, middle boy. He looked like me, just like me when I stared at the work-cracked hands of my mother, more than fifty years earlier—weary, curious and transported.

The reason that he held on to his relationship with Hind, he thought, was that he did not know exactly what happened between them, where it was leading him, or what she desired from it all. Maybe it was for this reason that he preserved his role in their relationship as a silent listener. He was excited by the idea that she had spent long years in camps with combatants and on battlefields, before she arrived here to talk bitterly about how they no longer write good theatre roles for women, then to go on judging him for the fact that he was not angry enough.

He sat in front of her with curious eyes. Between them was a tray that held two cups of coffee and an ashtray full to the brim with cigarette butts, mostly streaked by red lipstick.

She told endless stories, as he struggled to control his imagination, to keep it from straying to other scenes—this became harder as their sessions grew longer and more numerous.

She looked strong, with a taut body and exhausted eyes. It started there, in the power emitted by her taut body, the surge of her chest and the firmness of her breasts. Then her obscene laugh, the direct speech and the curses that flashed in her speech like a linked chain of spontaneous parentheticals.

Sometimes he thinks that it all came down to her dialect, a confused mix based in the Damascene, speckled always with shadows of meaning and metaphors hinted at by stray letters and echoed syllables. The dialect reminded him of Arab kasbahs, closed lanes and the fortified windows of old Damascus houses. Within outer walls, behind thick hedges of Jasmine and stained glass, the language had carved out its metaphors, rendering sensations through additions of sound that in turn bore deep suggestions, prayers engendered in, and depending on, interpretation. It seemed to him that these instruments had been polished, honed, perfected and practised through ages of contemplation in the dark, behind fences and sheltered windows, in practises of mastery behind covers and black sheets.

Damascus no longer resembled itself, but the dialect remained firm, calling, lithe, quick, slipping beyond enclosures, then tightening as it climbed into the mountains, gaining sternness and austerity, sounds following the enunciations of the letters that shortened like fast carriages loaded with dark promise. The male accent was boisterous and confident, full of pretensions to power, like a crude and unconvincing objection. In its layers of performance, there was a gathering attempt to confirm not mere control, but an absolute truth, the attempt to seize upon a truth as it collapsed completely, behind the thick curtains and ornate window blinds, behind the locked doors and fences, amid scents of jasmine, translucent seeping fabrics—muslin especially. The dialect flitted and lightened like some visionary whisper, emitting promises against the curves of a body, producing exquisite temptations.

There, too, was a strand of the light, agile, compliant Lebanese dialect, endlessly stringing parentheticals that consigned the cargo of thought in speech that never renounced the habitual and the commonly exchanged. Here the eclecticism of the Syrian dialects faded out, in overlapping levels of speech that included nearly everything, from direct figuration to minor asides dispatched to render and magnify the meaning.

What struck him first in his return were the dialects and the roads. It mystified him that he belonged to none of these. The dialects emerged from the villages with their successively differing rhythms and alterations, the thickening and submergence of the *kaaf*, the lightening of the *qaaf* until it touched the *kaaf*. These observations lured him into long, open conversations with taxi drivers and vegetable sellers. The variations between the dialect from the furthest south in Gaza, which carried the rhythms of the Egyptian but did not have the gaiety and smoothness of the decisive and smooth speech in Cairo, which seemed to glide effortlessly along through passing metaphors with the force of collectively affirmed symbols. In contrast, here, the language was thick and mixed with strands from the talk of the bedouins, which always implied doubt but never fully offered negation. The Gazan dialect, he thought, bended and gazed towards Egypt with a fixed stance. This, he thought, showed the difference between the dialects of coastal cities and those of the mountain towns, such as Hebron, where the dialect, hidden behind reeds, brimmed with spilling elongation and amplification, where words were given their fullest space, where letters opened themselves into long vowels and glottal stops, and consonants were endowed with their fully saturated cadence.

He was seduced into observing the conversations of people, as he wondered at the relaxation with which they uttered the dialects in all their strange diversity, as he himself stumbled through his hybrid dialect, which showed him always, at first utterance, to be a person returning. His return became a place that he could add to all the others.

Rising towards Jerusalem, it feels as if you pulled a heavy load up from a deep well, or dragging a silent league of white hills behind you, as you climb the road paved by the Turks at the beginning of the last century, from Jericho to Jerusalem, passing by Tayyebe and its church of Saint George, Saint Khodor as the Muslims call him, where the festival was held to celebrate the beer produced at the brewery in town.

Then the road continues its cautious ascent through narrow and dangerous zigzags, making cross-sections of the mountain and following the cracks of the earth.

An unfinished network of crumbling, abandoned pedestrian trenches and barren salt formations appears below. There is a cracked and rusted helmet of a Jordanian soldier, amid everything else left by the sons of the bedouins and the Jahili Arabs who gathered the telephone wires, rainwater, empty ammunition boxes, cassettes, epaulettes, belts and medals of fallen soldiers, within a scene bearing witness to a war no longer remembered.

In the remotest depths of the two wadis, machine skeletons lie like forsaken gifts, alone and defeated, like bodies whose souls have departed with no mention and no ceremony, no flowers, no muttering of the Fatiha in the dry abyss.

The dilapidated trenches and passages for lone pedestrians, are faded, overtaken by war, by front lines and aeroplanes, as the rise towards Ramallah continues. Then the gates of Jerusalem and the encircling settlement walls appear.

The story of Palestine was hidden inside the roads, he thought, where the depth and necessity of things appear, where cold description was overturned, yielding to a depth found in trails that connect, vectors passing through the mountains and strange wadis. It was not the quest for exaggerated aesthetics of poets and romantic novelists, but a scene of painful, violent, uncontrolled energy, cold and bitter directions that course through astonishing, contradictory forms, forging ways through the alloy of fear, belief, rebellion, contentment and self-annihilation. The lote tree of the lowlands connected to the olive tree of the hills. All this confusion, he thought, was like some rough draft of wisdom thrown on the shoulders of this country.

The roads stunned him when he first returned to Palestine. Since that summer evening in 1994, he did not go where his memory would have led him, back to that small two-storey house on the downslope in Beit Jala.

That was where he was born and spent his earliest years. Nothing remained of it now except a blurred scene of happiness, running through the rain pouring in an olive grove.

His return was, at first, like that of some curious tourist, or a tentative venture into political exile on the way towards some other, final exile. He saw as much as he could, adding to his spare and simple notes, his devices for contemplation and the relinquishing of the present, in order to keep the place from transforming entirely into a painful ambush of fear. This was why he was so persistent in his contemplation of all these things.

Now, as if in some renewal of his adventure, he ascended the hills that encircled Birzeit. He saw the university buildings and the murky shadows of the forests, and the minarets of the small villages that climbed the steep slopes of the hills. Settlement walls appeared like cold reptiles on the hills' shoulders. He contemplated the effect of the road between Ramallah and Birzeit, that it could arouse and cultivate surprise, even now, ten years after that evening when he first arrived to Birzeit.

At the beginning, the turns of the road and the small houses amid bits of greenery all caused small outpourings of astonishment, maybe because of his fear of what had not yet occurred. Perhaps he was afraid at what the scenes of his exile might add to these reappearing possessions that were somehow almost his.

He tried to hold on to the idea that he had finally reached some earthly place. He knew that he could not now, or ever, dissolve his attachment to this unfinished, poor road, marked in so many places by checkpoints and inspection points, by cement blocks and sudden potholes, this beaten road that was permanently exposed to the interferences and enterprises of others. The double turnoff at Mount Najma, too, had the power to cause a jolt of surprise, like the breaking of a continuous daily routine.

The road itself had become an event, and all simple and spontaneous relations were dissolved. He could no longer stop and ask questions, inside this event that was separated from all description and geography.

By now he knew all of its details, he could precisely delineate its pits and potholes, the points where the soldiers liked to erect their checkpoints, the turns, the thresholds of houses and shops, and the sudden rushes of cats and bodies that leapt from positions almost at random from both sides, the postures of men and boys who stared for no reason, without anger or contentment, as if he had cancelled their vision by some inappropriate passage.

He stared at their hands, which rose by some fine mechanism in memorized operations, as if giving greetings to the air, signals that had to be dismantled and linked somehow to coordinates of time, place and eye contact, and rebuilt into 'Good morning', 'Peace upon you' or 'Happy Birthday'.

Neutrally, they lifted their hands and looked through eyes that he did not know. The stopping and staring of the eyes was familiar, something like an obliged performance or the pursuit of some reward. It must be some kind of work, he thought, this fishing for reward or planting of 'trust.' But what it produced was only a silent field.

He searched for their hands in the darkness, as he returned, exhausted. They rose, shy and hesitant, more like a wish than a demand for pause or contact. When he asked,

'Where to?' an eternal answer came,

'Here.'

Those who pass in the night are now *here*.

Here extended towards him, as he ascended, as the companion became the intended place. *Here* disintegrated and became an agreed, functioning signal, as if to say without reason,

'Towards home.'

He went to the village of Jibiya. On the new farm road, passing by the houses of Barham and the shrine erected for its guardian, he looked towards the deep wadis and saw deer, feeling lucky to catch their anxious shadows flitting across lines of olive trees and over stubborn mountain plants.

From the highest point, the tremendous network of small roads appeared, trod by feet, cutting through the western mountain chain. The maze of trails and pathways between towns, villages and houses, proceeded in a preordained agreement towards Jerusalem.

As if to complement the surging and deep fervour of the earth, the roads on these mountains formed a narrative fitted to the place, bending through descents as if afraid to wound the earth or tear the folds of its ancient body.

The road bended around a tree, encircled a boulder, then stopped completely before the threshold of a house.

Within the story, the roads took up only what was needed for breath and passage.

To one returning to this country, the roads were the most important part of earth. They were more important than the houses, the forests and the wadis with their strange names. Wadis were transformed into roads and passages. The Wadi of Fire which is not the Wadi of Hell mentioned by Ibn Battuta in his journey to Jerusalem, as was long thought. The downslope and steep ascent between Jericho and Bethlehem, after the turn towards Jerusalem, then the final summit where the breath became short. The people and the mountains, the caravans, then the monastery in Abdiyya, silent and still like a stone miracle. Wadi Qelt, which fell ruggedly from the flank of Jerusalem and channelled the waters of fading springs into the Jordan River as it passed Jericho, where the monks dug their monasteries into stone on the bank of the river's course in their eternal wake. The Wadi of Thieves, going north towards Nablus, twisting around the abandoned station of the Jordanian police, where a sergeant had once been stationed, some thirty years ago, and officers looked for bandits over the tops of the stones. Where had they gone?

Far off, on the bluffs of south-facing mountains, smoke rose from small villages, mixing with the vapours of the bushes and the dark vegetation. He continued his descent, surrounded by short forest trees and thorny plants. He saw minarets, church spires and monasteries, and traces of abandoned houses.

Something was different. The scent of silence and betrayal, giving its character to the houses. A piece of broken glass in a doorway. Someone telling you, someone describing. An energy of description, fleeting signals in the air that grant you the power to tell apart those houses, to know and name them, signals leading to regions submerged in detail. Suddenly you see the houses in front of you whose families left them in haste: the astonishment of windows, belongings, pictures, clothes and the open door of the cupboard, a picture of a father or grandfather in the sitting-room chest. Small secrets divulged inside rooms, a rushed salutation to an iron bannister with its flaked-off paint.

The houses, he thought, are roads that had been intensified, reckoned, understood, inhabited, transformed into familiar passages. What remained free and solid was what could not be placated, what was left behind to lure us into pleasures and perils.

Houses are familiar roads, tamed, raised and taught to serve the family through perplexing human diligence. Houses are roads in cages, there is no doubt of that.

He thought about the roads, and the villages that appeared like discarded fruit on their edges. He thought about the doors that opened onto the asphalt. The doors were crude geometric extensions of the roads. It seemed that they were sleepwalking, nothing more.

Her Laugh That He Found Obscene

Over the course of long months, they would meet on the stairs up to the building. They would exchange greetings, and then turn to open the door to their flats. This was until a single instance, when he met her by chance at the entrance to the building surrounded by grocery bags. Politely and insincerely, he offered to help. She agreed right away and pointed to the pile of bags, then picked up some of them and went ahead of him. The bags did not feel as heavy as they had looked on the ground, and he remembered the thick scent of mint that flowed from them. He followed her up the few stairs to the second floor where she lived. At the entrance to her door, she laughed and invited him inside. It was that laugh that he found obscene.

This was the first time that he entered her flat. The layout was the same as his, with an entryway, sitting room and narrow kitchen that extended onto a balcony overlooking the main street, and her bed-room, behind a door with a low, wide window.

The walls of the sitting room were bare. There was a wide sofa in the corner, a bench and a table of black wood. On the bookshelf was an old edition of the poems of Mahmoud Darwish, and the novels of Ghassan Kanafani, who was assassinated by a car bomb in Beirut at the age of thirty-seven. Among these books, he could make out the title *Returning to Haifa*. Between the two of them was a wood panel displaying a popular commercial cartoon by Naji al-Ali, next to a picture of her in military clothes standing at the entrance to a bombed building.

On a small table next to the sofa, facing the TV-set, there was a picture of her standing next to a man on top of a boulder. She was in swimming clothes and the man was smiling towards the camera. She looked over the man's shoulder at the sea, and there was a small fishing boat in the background.

'This picture was taken in Saida. This is my husband.'

Her voice crossed the kitchen barrier, and she laughed again, the same laugh that he found obscene.

'He got away.'

At first, he could not understand what she meant by 'got away', or why she laughed. He thought that the man was dead and that she was trying to tell him that rather crudely.

'We separated. He refused the idea of returning here. He would repeat it always, without stopping, in the shower, in front of the window, in bed, in front of the TV screen, "Not like this, Hind. Not like this."

'I finally stopped trying to convince him, and we went silent. I was preparing my bags, and he went to the seashore to sit on the rock in this picture.' Then she added as she came across the barricade carrying a coffee tray, 'He stayed there with his mother, his memories and his tabby cat.'

It all felt shocking and abrupt to him. This is what she intended, he thought, to shove him by his shoulders into her life without preparation or invitation, without even a moment's time for him to show interest. It was strange and confusing, to attempt to reconcile between her tone which showed no loss or regret, and the fact that she had cherished the picture, a wonderful portrait of this man, he thought. The situation seemed to be one of irony and neutrality.

We Did Not Find the Railway Station

There were no Jews in his mother's stories until the appearance of the railway station, and Rivka who sat under the eucalyptus tree. Before that, they appeared only in the deaths and ruinous destinies of others: 'The Jews killed him', 'the Jews took him', 'the Jews burned him', 'the Jews kidnapped him'. They were there beyond the singular, as a mysterious, impenetrable mass yielding no singular entities. They all undertook the same work, moved in the same direction, chased, slept, spoke in one voice, pointed with one hand, breathed together. They wore a single mask. This seemed to have a relaxing effect, allowing antipathy and fear to be built collectively, to generate an energy for vengeance deeply reinforced by continual loss—a blind power that permitted no specification or exception, no power to pierce the mask.

Rivka's dissimilarity from the mask, owing to her Arab appearance, and the outstretched hand of the

nurse offering two pieces of candy to the two children in a countryside railway station, granted a power
of departure into thin air. A deep longing raised those
memories from the well of forgetting, and they stood
motionless at the edge of the station, untaken by the
disaster that occurred afterward.

His mother went along, without hesitation, with
the American journalist to Zakariyya.

She readied herself in the morning, in complete
silence, as if to keep an appointment.

He stayed back in the house so as not to com-
plicate things, especially since he did not have a permit. He waited anxiously for her return, calling the
journalist every ten minutes to check in on the
progress of the journey.

When she returned in the evening, she was calm.
She sat on the balcony, looking out on the windows
across the street, and said, 'We did not find the railway
station.'

The collapse of the story now intensified. The
absence of the railway station had a violent effect,
enough to erase everything, all the memories and
longing that it engendered. The Jewish girl now

stumbled through confused places and over obscure woodlands, falling continuously without end.

His mother died at the end of August in her house in Amman. He arrived too late to participate in the funeral ceremonies due to the long procedure of crossing the Bridge, as always. He sat in her room that same evening, after he had greeted and said goodbye to the consoling visitors. The picture of her in Bethlehem in the black dress hung on the wall, the one that Hind had faced when she said, 'You don't look like your mother.'

He did not look like her, he thought. He shared little with her, as it had always been. He tried to imagine her descending the woods towards the railway station, leading the family's horse. He could see her light reddish hair, her astonishment, her two small feet and the evident confidence in the simple way that she turned—confidence that she embodied even in her last days. It all ended here, even if it were repeated often.

He took with him the picture and one of her rosaries, the turquoise-blue one that he had brought her from Baghdad. With difficulty, he was led to her grave on the second day.

The cemetery was vast and maze-like. He thought of his father's grave on the mountain north of the city, poor and abandoned, which had been hard to find the few times he had visited. He saw the apparent, ardent care given to the grave of his mother, which was dug into the plot purchased by her family in the cemetery. It was surrounded by a small fence, with a gate, descending steps, and carefully tended oleander plants.

She had returned to her family, he thought. But then he felt, rather unexpectedly, that what she needed was to be led to the railway station. She needed the comfort of her narrative. But he could not give her that, and now it was no longer necessary.

Failure of the Old Man's Fourth Attempt

A young, armed intelligence agent, standing at the outer door, prevented him from returning inside. He seemed shocked and completely unconvinced by the idea of 'forgetting a book'. He tried to convince him of his need to retrieve the book, but he could not stomach entering disputes with this kind of armed rooster.

It felt as if he was seeing her naked when she came out of the glass cage. It was the first time that he had seen her in person. She was in her mid-thirties, and the intense outdoor light magnified the freckles on her cheeks and the uncovered part of her chest. She was shorter than she seemed inside the cage, and fuller, and she was carrying the book. From where he stood outside the glass door, he could read the title, *Farewell, Babylon*.

She stood behind the rooster. He could see the depth of the hall behind her, and the empty chair where the short young man had been sitting. In the depths, the old man was still shedding his clothing, and behind him the line of waiting people grew. It looked like a satirical cartoon depicting some improvised tragedy.

The rooster who had forbidden him from entering, relented and took the book from her hands. He started to leaf through it, attempting to appear ironical.

'Is this your book?'

He spoke in Hebrew. He could understand what was said, but when he tried to find an appropriate response, he could not.

Behind the rooster, he heard her voice say, also in Hebrew, 'He doesn't speak Hebrew.'

So the rooster asked him in English, 'What is in this book?'

The rooster, he thought, has no use for the Arabic language.

'A novel,' he replied.

'What does the novel say?'

'It narrates . . .'

'What does it say, your novel, about the Jews?'

'There are no Jews in this novel.'

'Novels with no Jews are usually boring.'

The rooster was trying to be clever. He thought about what he could say to this repulsive, armed youth, while also attempting to stay here longer so that he could look at her better. It was clear that the two of them were joined by the rooster and his repulsiveness as they held their glance. This was fairly evident, and also worrying. A fine line had been suddenly crossed, a departure from the main road off into some confused and utterly removed side trail.

The old man now stood like an angel in his white cotton undershirt. He looked thin, alone and strange. He had lost his earlier bearing and posture, the composure he held at when he left his house this morning had disintegrated past a point of no return. He shook his head constantly, looking down at his bare feet. He was withdrawn, no longer even slightly concerned with the response of the machine. He looked exhausted. The line behind him, the Arab worker, the woman soldier and the intelligence officer all tried to urge him to pass through again, but he kept shaking his head and locked his knees. He did not look at the woman soldier, the Arab worker or the intelligence man. He clearly did not hear the growing calls from the line behind him, and did not even look at the machine. He stood in his white underwear like an angel lost and devoid of purpose, banished from paradise, trying to remember some-thing, perhaps, that he might have lost, something that he might need but could not reclaim. Some field in his spirit had been corrupted.

'It is a very boring novel, then,' he replied to the rooster, taking the book from his hand. Then he turned around to get back on the bus.

The tall young man was still standing at the door of the bus, smoking and looking towards the entrance of the hall, as the driver turned the engine and started the air-conditioning. The driver placed his hand on the wheel, and glanced at the empty seats at the back. The fat man was taking things out of a backpack. The family had spread out into the row of seats to the right and Yusuf, who was under control now, was crumpled in exhaustion on his father's lap. The objecting young girl in jeans was trying to make a call on her mobile phone. He chose a new seat. Through the window he could see her at the entrance. She was looking at the bus as the rooster tried to draw her attention, swaying and pointing at him as he spoke, no doubt still talking about him. He could not let go of the painful scene of the old man in front of the machine, and a sense of guilt started to grow. He tried to let it go but the idea that he had been so taken with her, so eager to fall into her snares, and the short conversation they exchanged, it all filled him with a desire for her that he could no longer ignore. The desire seemed to liberate him from the thought of the old man, to allow him to forget him there in front of the machine. It felt like a painful betrayal.

She knocked on the door, then pushed it open. She wore a black-and-white sweatsuit and her hair was tied in a ponytail.

'I heard the sound of the TV and thought you were awake.'

'I didn't sleep well. They are bombing Gaza.'

Without a pause, she said, 'My water is cut off.'

He didn't understand.

She continued.

'Can I take a quick shower at your place?'

He said, 'Of course.'

'I will get my things.'

She turned back towards her flat.

It was a big step forward, he thought, but there was nothing in her face or voice to indicate that she was interested in anything else, nothing in the words to give rise to any other interpretation.

He hopped into the bathroom to make sure it was clean. Traces of the morning shower were still there, the towel and shaving instruments spread on the sink in front of the mirror, a scent of cologne, and an open shower curtain. He could not keep himself from imagining her naked body, surrounded by her things, standing in the bathtub and rubbing her small, firm, dark body. The trembling of her soft breasts rendered the scene complete.

He had never made an approach, because he feared her power and the torrent that ruled her movements, and because he feared the implications of the fulfilment that could come with that approach, that he would then not be as independent as he had planned. He knew that this was not the kind of woman who knocked on the door before entering, that she would invade the furthest regions of his life. She would place her clothes in the dresser and her make-up and toothbrush in the bathroom drawer. She would fiddle with his pictures and books, and pose so many unexpected questions—as she always did. She is an actress, that is what she does and she is good at it, he thought, even if he had never seen her on stage. She was a fighter, even if she never talked about it. She was spontaneous and beautiful, and afraid of getting older alone, although she never mentioned it. Somewhere in her voice she was hurried and confused. He loved and yearned for her small body, which he also feared. He returned to the thought of her occasional visitor, who seemed like one of the wizened government employees, and whom he did not dare to ask about until now.

He heard the sound of the door as it opened, and her voice as she entered. He felt her breathing and the presence of her body behind him as he tried to gather his shaving instruments from the edge of the sink. She held a small bag and a beach towel. 'Leave everything where it is,' she said, 'I won't take more than ten minutes.'

He went to the living room while she opened her small bag.

He heard the pouring of the water and tried to keep her wet body from his imagination.

On the screen in front of him, ambulances rushed forth with their back doors flung open, as the camera raced through dark, dusty alleys, lights flashed over terrified feet sprinting in plastic sandals through Gaza's shattered alleys.

'The first time that I met Ali, I was getting out of the bath.' Ali must be her former husband, he thought, the man with the light hair that he saw in the photo, who sat on the boulder and smiled to the camera. 'I had rented a room from his mother in the camp.' Hind continued, 'It was a small room on the roof of their house, at the end of a staircase that we shared. The room had a window overlooking the orchards that stretched along the length of the coast, a blue, wooden window with a rattan seat facing it, and a military bed. The room was clean, and so were the sheets on the bed. The staircase ended in a narrow landing, and the bathroom was on the other side, a narrow square of Chinese tiles, a white basin surrounded by a curtain, and water that would creep into the room every time I washed. I was coming out of the bath, as I told you, when he knocked at the door, and said, "I am your neighbour, Umm Ali's son. If you need anything from Beirut, tell me. I go there every day except Sunday."

'He was good, direct and concise. I thought that his hair was thinning and that he would lose it before he turned forty, and that our children would inherit that trait if we married. He had not hinted at anything. It was the first time I saw him, but still I imagined him in my bed, with his short body and thin hair. I could see a place for his eyeglasses on the commode, next to the picture of Guevara.

'We married some months later, and we stayed in the same room. He did not bring anything. His clothes remained in his mother's closet, with his books and the Egyptian TV series that he loved. Only the cat followed him to join us in that small room. He was good, and I was content. It was like a game of husband and wife, and it suited everyone— me, him and his mother.

'I remember once he asked me about my family. I told him about the dozens of children who died from malaria, snakebites and scorpions in the Jordan Valley, where the ground fell to its lowest depth, where we lived below the sea level, our eyes distracted by the lights of Jericho and the sun's reflection off the Dead Sea; and about the mist that covered the hills of Jerusalem above us, before an armed Israeli division crossed the river and wiped out the camp.

'We fled to the mountains through rough wadis, and from there we were scattered across distant camps in the east, or further still in Syria, or further in Lebanon. So many collapsed during the journey, and mothers, fathers and brothers separated. But as I spoke to Ali, I noticed he was not paying attention, but was staring at me with wide eyes as if he were looking through me. I kept telling the story, some kind of unknown stubbornness pressed me. Something let me keep on telling the story even if he never paid any attention. He seemed to ignore them, the people flooding across the mountains on their defeated journey who kept creeping over the highlands and harsh trails pulling children and their belongings. He kept on staring at nothing, and I continued.

'I have a brother who is older. He disappeared in the Israeli raid on Lebanon in the summer of 1982. We don't really know what happened to him. Someone confirmed that he was killed, and someone else added that they buried him in the grave of numbers. "You know about the grave of numbers, Ali?"

'He wasn't paying attention, so I continued.

'There is one at the Bridge of Jacob's Daughters that contains five hundred graves. Each of its burial mounds has a metal sign bearing a number, with no crosses or crescents or even gravestones, just metal

139

signs, most of them consumed by rust, and faded numbers. No "One who believes in me, even if he perishes, shall live", no Fatiha, no "O soul find contentment, and return to your Lord contented". Just the number. No visitors, no flowers, no reciters, nothing of this kind. Five hundred are decomposing there under the poor mounds with no names above them, only their file numbers.

'There are other graves, too, which journalists, probably Israelis, have discovered. Like us, they cannot figure out why the punishment of these people had to continue, why their bodies and names were obliterated, why they were thrown into this strange confinement. I am sure that my brother can be found in the one at the Bridge of Jacob's Daughters. They say that most of the five hundred in that mass grave were killed in the attack on Lebanon in the summer of 1982. My brother was there, in Tyre. The last time I saw him, he took me to a small restaurant on the beach. It was a hut erected on the edge of the water, not a restaurant exactly. We ate fried fish. He had to return to his studies a few weeks later, when his training period was ending. He introduced me to his friends. One of them was a Lebanese girl named

Maryam. On the way back, I took his clothes to wash, some books and a list of books that I was supposed to find for him in Beirut.'

She stopped speaking for a moment. When she did start talking again, he did not know if she was speaking to the man in the picture on the sea, or to him.

'I have a lawyer now,' she said quietly.

He thought, that must be the man who visited her regularly each week, whom he had met once or twice at the entrance to the flat. He seemed to be nice, in his fifties, like one of those peaceful government employees.

'We are trying, a number of families and myself, to build a legal suit, to bring the children back from those graves. We have been trying for three years. There are so many of them, so many graves. Egyptian, Palestinian, Lebanese, Syrian, Jordanian, Moroccan and Kurds.'

As she went on speaking, he thought of a rare picture taken by a journalist of one of these graves. For some reason, he thought it must have been the one near the Bridge of Jacob's Daughters. The faded picture showed the mounds of the abandoned graves, and the number plates. In the foreground of the picture was the Number 44. Plate Number 201 had fallen on the ground, to the left of 44. A bent sign hung at the bottom of the frame, and at the top of the picture was a number eaten by rust which for some reason he guessed was 236. He could not stop thinking about that bent sign, and the decaying number that tried to raise its head to utter 236.

'So I stopped talking. I noticed that I was getting angry, which was surprising. I didn't recall us ever really differing. He accepted everything and so did I, except for that night. Even when I told him that I was going to return, he seemed to have expected it. At first, he was silent, then he said, "As for me, I cannot. We are from Safed. I cannot leave my mother alone. We will remain refugees in Ramallah." That night, as he undressed me, I continued, "I will not leave my mother to die alone in the camp."

'On the morning of my travel, he had left before I woke up. He had gone to the beach, as always, to calm his nerves. I thought about following him, but I was prevented by a short note that he had left on the pillow. It was written with a dry ballpoint pen.

The letter had eight words, two sentences, "As I said, I cannot. Not like this."

'The pillow was white with light-blue stripes, and the letter looked like a fragment of dream that had fallen out of our sleep.'

She was in front of the bookshelves. A lock of her wet hair showed under the beach towel wrapped around her head. Beads flowed under her thin white shirt, causing it to stick to her chest. This woman had a need, he thought, for someone like him, someone who could listen. His importance was that he could listen to her stories, he thought, and he did love this, he loved her way of telling, of summoning persons through riveting, sung intonations in the layers of her voice and eyes, in the re-creation of the dialect of the people in her stories. Sometimes, she would stand up to perform or imitate someone. They could all be brought forth at her beckoning. When she had finished a story, she would go back to gather them, to snatch them from the air of the room and whisk them through the floating smell of cardamom coffee, then return them to the distant places that she protected with passion.

'Have you read all these books?'

'No.'

'Then why do you keep them?'

'To read them.'

'Where are the books you have read?'

'Friends took them.'

'Have you read this?'

'Not completely.'

'It seems complex.'

'Yes, I think so.'

She still had her back to him, and her eyes on the shelves of books. Her back was wet, and the dark colour of her taut skin showed clearly under the light fabric. Then her shoulders flowed as she lowered herself, with confidence, into the tub. The small mirror that she had propped on the shelf accidentally reflected her firm backside, the rise of her breast under the wet fabric and her nipple. Her bare feet had traced a path on the bare tiles. He followed the path. He put his arms around her, he heard her breathe deeply. The scent of the wet body that now held him. When he embraced her, she seemed shorter, smaller, more fragile, and there was a lamenting, ceaseless sigh in her breathing. It passed from her shoulders to her hands, to her fingers, like a light carriage with wings.

Sounds of children and cars arrived from the street, then the call of the baker, and a woman called out for Ismail. That must be the grocer's thin, blonde son, he guessed.

She lit a cigarette from her pack and handed it to him with her eyes closed. Her lips were open, and small beads of sweat flashed on her upper lip. Her face seemed to relax as they smoked together in silence, lying naked on the floor. After a long silence she said,

'This was necessary.' Then she added, 'I needed that.'

He made no comment, but tried to recall her body, the degree of her trembling, the firmness of her breasts, to unravel her astonishment and the strange silence as she held him. He knew now that she was beautiful and, despite everything, she was also reserved. He desired that always.

The broadcaster on Al-Jazeera was putting emotional questions to an Israeli officer about the assassination of three youths in Gaza. She held his hand

and kissed the centre of the palm, then rested it on her chest. He heard her breathe as she turned towards him.

The Moroccan Woman's Coffee Shop

He kept returning to Zakariyya whenever he had the opportunity, often by sneaking his way back. He would stop at the small, surprising coffee shop at the turn to the road that led from the village towards Jerusalem.

He went to the coffee shop to stare at the trees and listen to the longing of its owner for her past in Marrakech—which he relished whenever he went.

'You look like a Moroccan.'

She always repeated, sitting next to him and resuming her hobby of speaking Arabic in her anxious Marrakech dialect. She seemed to recall the dialect better each time.

There was some confused apology in her speech as they sat at the table facing the pine forest. Every now and then, the whiff of the sea would arrive from beyond the hills, military vehicles would stop, troops would come over for coffee, and sit at the neighbouring tables. A bewildered apology limped through the lingering Arabic words in her memory, a language that had decayed and left only the dialect alive. The dialect was stronger, it had more power to remain.

This woman was trying to apologize, he liked to think, so that she could continue to sit in front of the forest contented, happily deploying the movements of her body. She was using him and his seemingly neutral act of listening, he thought, to renew her contentment at the fact that she was here, not he nor his mother nor Rivka. Her confused apology, he thought, like her stumbling Arabic, served to fortify and preserve this contentment. He liked to think that Hind might have been thinking about all this when she said to him, looking at the picture of his mother,

'You do not look like your mother . . . You are not angry enough.'

By this time, he had altogether stopped asking about the railway station, so he had not thought to ask the Moroccan woman about it. It seemed that the matter was out of his hands now, that it was no longer possible to rebuild the story or work with it.

He preferred to sit where he could look out towards the main street and the downsloping forest, watching the pines lean into the wadi. This was the same table where he had been with Hasan the driver who brought him from Gaza to Ramallah the first time, who continued to pass between endlessly shifting border guards, climbing from the south towards the mountains of Jerusalem, or descending the low-lying dunes at the edges of the Sinai. But this afternoon, a group of tourists had occupied that table when he arrived, and the Moroccan woman, who met him on the step of the narrow wooden bridge, pointed him instead to the empty table to the left. She went ahead of him to open the window, speaking to him in her own strange Arabic. It was then that he first caught sight, through the open window, of the abandoned station and the railway track. Grass had grown in the spaces between the tracks, climbing over the edges of the rusted iron seats. Old, untended Kenya trees made the sight dark and imposing. On the wall of the abandoned guard room, an election poster of a candidate wearing a kippah had been washed by rain into streaks of blue.

He became aware that the entire coffee shop was built inside disused train carriages that the Moroccan woman had converted to her residence and the coffee shop. He saw now that the Moroccan woman, the Palestinian waiter behind the bar, the group of German tourists and the arriving soldiers were all sitting inside his mother's memory. They were inside a snapshot of the nurse extending her hand, descending from the train with two candies in her hand for two girls, one of whom was her daughter.

The Moroccan woman took him by the hand to the carriage at the end of the hall. There was a bed behind the bar and a shelf of books above it. In the opposite corner was a mirror, next to a small table covered by decorative objects, powders, bottles of perfume and hairbrushes. She opened a side door, and descended two steps of heavy wood, then went out with him into the station.

He walked on the rusted tracks, as if stumbling against the catastrophe and his mother's death on the east of the river.

The dry grass broke audibly under his feet and stuck to his shins. The Moroccan woman stood on the thick wooden steps, with dyed hair, bracelets encircling her wrists. She looked at him, in silence, as if watching the arrival of a funeral procession of ghosts. The old, empty carriages of stories seemed to breathe. The curtains shook in his mother's memory, quivering with the force of her strange anxiety about the railway track. His father seemed to step from a train carriage, and walked towards the house through the forest's leaning pines.